W9-CDZ-965

"IT'S THE CAT'S PAJAMAS." ***—Tulsa World***

More praise for Lydia Adamson's Alice Nestleton Mysteries . . .

"Witty . . . slyly captivating."

—*Publishers Weekly*

"Smooth prose and a clever plot."

—*Library Journal*

"Just plain fun." —*Painted Rock Reviews*

"Cat lovers will no doubt exult . . . charming sketches of the species." —*Kirkus Reviews*

"A blend of the sublime with a tinge of suspense as Alice, like her four-pawed friends, uses her uncanny intuition to solve a baffling mystery." —*Mystery Reviews*

"Whimsical. Lifts readers out of the doldrums with cheery characters who steal the show."

—*Midwest Book Review*

"An ideal stocking stuffer for cat-doting mystery fans."

—*Roanoke Times*

"Cleverly written, suspenseful . . . the perfect gift for the cat lover." —*Lake Worth Herald*

Other Books in the Alice Nestleton Mystery Series

A CAT IN THE MANGER

A CAT OF A DIFFERENT COLOR

A CAT IN WOLF'S CLOTHING

A CAT BY ANY OTHER NAME

A CAT IN THE WINGS

A CAT WITH A FIDDLE

A CAT IN A GLASS HOUSE

A CAT WITH NO REGRETS

A CAT ON THE CUTTING EDGE

A CAT ON A WINNING STREAK

A CAT IN FINE STYLE

A CAT IN A CHORUS LINE

A CAT UNDER THE MISTLETOE

A CAT ON A BEACH BLANKET

A CAT ON JINGLE BELL ROCK

A CAT ON STAGE LEFT

A CAT OF ONE'S OWN

A Cat with the Blues

An Alice Nestleton Mystery

Lydia Adamson

SIGNET
Published by New American Library, a division of
Penguin Putnam Inc., 375 Hudson Street,
New York, New York 10014, U.S.A.
Penguin Books Ltd, 27 Wrights Lane,
London W8 5TZ, England
Penguin Books Australia Ltd,
Ringwood, Victoria, Australia
Penguin Books Canada Ltd, 10 Alcorn Avenue,
Toronto, Ontario, Canada M4V 3B2
Penguin Books (N.Z.) Ltd, 182–190 Wairau Road,
Auckland 10, New Zealand

Penguin Books Ltd, Registered Offices:
Harmondsworth, Middlesex, England

First published by Signet, an imprint of New American Library,
a division of Penguin Putnam Inc.

Printed in the United States of America

PUBLISHER'S NOTE
This is a work of fiction. Names, characters, places, and incidents either are the product of the author's imagination or are used fictitiously, and any resemblance to actual persons, living or dead, business establishments, events, or locales is entirely coincidental.

ISBN 0-7394-1403-8

Chapter 1

After twenty minutes of wandering through the immense office supply store on Fifty-seventh Street—the flagship in a citywide chain of such stores—attempting to follow the logic of the aisle signs, I gave up.

I walked over to a handsome young man in a red blazer and asked, "Where are the large rubber bands?"

He was reflective.

"I mean the ones that come in many bright colors," I added. "Do you know the ones I'm talking about? I haven't been able to find them anywhere. But I know you carry them. I bought some last year in one of your downtown stores."

He began humming a tune I recognized immediately: "The Sidewalks of New York." I always seem to end up with the deranged service people. My luck was holding. This young fellow was absolutely buggy.

"Aisle three," he finally said.

"I've been to aisle three, young man," I said. "They aren't there." I had suddenly become suspicious of this character. Young men do not hum "The Sidewalks of New York." It's a very old tune, dating back, I think, to the turn of the century.

The salesman stared at me. I suppose he was trying to decide whether I was as loony as he. Then he motioned for me to follow him. We arrived at aisle three and he pointed out the rubber bands, not even bothering to look where he was pointing.

"Are these by any chance what you mean by 'rubber bands,' miss?" he asked, deadpan.

Well, there they were in plain sight. How could I have missed them? But before I could apologize for troubling him, he had walked away.

I picked up a packet and studied it. The colorful bands came twelve to the packet—nice sturdy long ones, at least six inches unstretched. And the colors were fine and dandy. Sunny yellow, ruby red, and French blue.

Dandy? Why had I used that extremely old-fashioned word? No one used dandy in that context anymore. No one used it at all.

Be careful, Alice, I warned myself. You won't be able to audition for lusty, hip wench parts anymore. Your language will blow your cover and tell your age.

I grinned. I never got those roles even when I was the right age.

Fine and dandy!

I selected two packages (after all, the prices here were discounted) and headed for the checkout counter.

There was a long line. Now that was odd: When I had entered the store, it seemed to be empty in spite of the fact that it was lunch hour on a weekday—and a lovely one in June, at that—and the neighborhood was filled with office workers.

How could the checkout line be so long when the store had virtually no customers on the floor?

That paradox was never solved. I tapped my foot impatiently as the line moved ever so slowly. I didn't know why I was getting so anxious. It was only a few minutes past noon and I was not due at my cat-sitting assignment, only a few blocks north of the store, until one.

The rubber bands were not for me but for my charge—Frenchy. She was a lovely Russian blue lady. I was bringing them to her in hopes of weaning her away from her toy mice, which she was shredding at an alarming rate. She was systematically destroying all ten of them, all sizes and shapes, and I thought the colorful, bouncy, and nearly indestructible rubber bands would make a great substitute. My own cats loved the things. They swatted them around with great glee. Why not Frenchy? She was a perfectly normal feline.

What wasn't so normal were the circumstances of this particular cat-sitting assignment. In fact, it was just about the most bizarre job I'd ever had—and certainly the most lucrative.

Sidney and Beatrice Woburn had been happily married for thirty-one years and had two grown children. He was a successful printer. She was a well-known craftsperson whose specialty was creating rugs, shawls, and kimonos that were meant to be displayed rather than put to practical use. The Woburns lived in a magnificent apartment on the twenty-sixth floor of the ASCAP building, across from Lincoln Center.

But somehow, for reasons unknown, the long and happy marriage had fallen apart. And the breakup was ugly and violent.

In fact, the situation was so bad that the respective lawyers had agreed on a simple solution to enforce a temporary truce: The couple would abandon the apartment altogether until a divorce agreement was reached.

Every book, vase, fork, lamp, and stick of furniture must remain inviolate because every single item was being contested.

And the central bone of contention was poor Frenchy. Both Woburns wanted her. Both were scheming to get her.

And so it was also decided that Frenchy should remain in the apartment with the other contested items, and each party would contribute to a seven-day-a-week cat-sitter. That turned out to be me.

I was being paid an astonishing amount of money for visiting Frenchy each day and seeing to her needs. I was required to remain with her for at least an hour and forty-five minutes a day. The husband and wife were allowed to visit her twice a week, separately of course, and only when I was present, so there would be no chance of either of them absconding with the cat.

It was the only time I was ever required to sign a contract for cat-sitting services. The contract was for six weeks and the signing was done in the presence of both parties and their attorneys: Paulus Darien for Sidney and A.G. Roth for Beatrice.

I was now in the third week of the contract, and to be quite truthful, other than the grim-faced visits to Frenchy by Sidney and Beatrice, the deal was fine . . . fine and dandy.

I didn't have much else to do anyway. Tony Basillio, my on-again off-again—but mostly on—companion, was teaching a course in stage design at a small college near Boston. He was sending me absentminded love letters while, no doubt, cruising the bars for ingenues.

My good friend Nora Karroll was on Martha's Vineyard, searching for a summer rental.

And my occasional associate in matters investigative, that genial wreck of a man and sometime author Samuel Tully, was chained to his typewriter, updating *Murders in the Rue Morgue* to a 1990s setting.

My own little career was on perma-hold, it seemed. And I desperately needed the money.

Two more registers had opened and the long line of customers dispersed. A few minutes later I was walking out of the store and heading uptown.

Since it was such a lovely day, I strolled through Central Park, exiting at Tavern on the Green, only a few blocks from my destination.

The moment I walked into the building, I began to look for Elias Almodovar. He was a substitute doorman working only three days a week. I had bumped into him in the lobby during my first week of cat-sitting Frenchy.

One of the joys of being an actress in New York is that you meet old acquaintances everywhere, anywhere, suddenly. They pop up under the most peculiar circumstances. Never in a million years would I have predicted that Elias Almodovar would be working as a part-time doorman, spiffy outfit and all. Nor could he envision me as a cat-sitter, he said.

Elias was a small, frail-looking, handsome man with enormous talent. He had appeared in several grim prison dramas in the 1970s—plays such as *Fortune and Men's Eyes.* Those roles got him noticed but also typecast him.

When the grim prison genre collapsed in the '80s, Elias found the going difficult, to say the least. He was too old, as he said, to join the *West Side Story* touring circus. Besides, he couldn't dance.

When we met that first day in the lobby, we hadn't seen each other in at least ten years. And I looked forward to seeing him every time I walked into the building. We would reminisce, gossip, and even cry a little.

That day he was not on duty. The regular doorman greeted me and handed me a note. It was a single typed sheet in a plain envelope. Enclosed was a check.

I read the epistle in the elevator:

Dear Miss Nestleton,

Frenchy's birthday is in two days' time. I have ordered her present from Dino's on 74th &

Amsterdam: 24 cans of Progresso tuna in olive oil. Please go there after leaving Frenchy today and pay with this check. They will deliver on her birthday.

Thank you,
Beatrice Woburn
P.S. Check for $71.76 enclosed.

That's a lot of tuna, I thought, but I was careful not to judge the gift, since I myself get rather bizarre birthday treats for my felines—such as saffron rice for Pancho.

I entered the apartment and was, as usual, struck by the waste of it all. For the huge, perfectly appointed apartment was deserted except for Frenchy. I mean, it was such a marvelous, comfortable place that I couldn't help wishing to see humans materialize and resume living in it.

Frenchy was on the arm of the sofa, her favorite roost. On one of the sofa cushions were two toy mice; one had red ears and a bell on its tail.

Frenchy gave me her usual acknowledgment—opening one eye and raising it a bit. She was a detached, sophisticated lady cat. Nothing much seemed to excite her except toy mice. And nothing much seemed to bother her either, except being picked up from behind. She had scratched me once when I tried it, and even gotten Beatrice Woburn on the neck when she attempted it during one of her visits.

Both scratches were small, luckily. Frenchy had delivered them almost lackadaisically.

Anyway, on that day I did my usual chores—refilling the cat's food dish, cleaning the litter box, gathering all the toy mice into one location, and so on. Then I decided to brush her. Frenchy, as usual, offered no resistance. On the other hand, she did not appear to enjoy it particularly either. Actually I was the one doing the enjoying, because Russian blues have essentially two coats: the outer one, although short-haired, is rather silky, but the inner coat is thick and resistant. This unique arrangement was, I imagine, an evolutionary adaption to the cold. After all, Russian blues are thought to have originated in the tundras and forests of Siberia, where they were hunted for fur. Supposedly they became extinct in the nineteenth century except for a few individuals of the domestic variety that were smuggled out by English sailors.

They recovered as a distinct breed in Great Britain in the early twentieth century, modified by Siamese bloodlines. The modern Russian blue has the same beautiful gray-blue coat as its ancestors but is much slimmer in build.

Of course, some people claim the Russian blue

is not Russian at all but of Swedish extraction. I am not qualified to say. And I couldn't care less.

Anyway, after I finished the brushing, I proceeded to my basic instructional class for felines in the theory and practice of rubber bands.

I slipped a green one surreptitiously out of the packet and kept it in the palm of my hand. Frenchy, after she was groomed, ate a bit of food, then hunted and mauled one of her mice, then took a postprandial stroll around the big apartment, and finally hopped back up on the arm of the sofa and closed her eyes.

I knew very well, or at least I believed it to be true, that all cats can see with their eyes closed. I jiggled the large rubber band in front of her closed eyes. No response.

I jiggled again. The eyes remained closed, but I could see her ears perk up a little.

I held the rubber band about six inches over her head and shook it hard. It danced and bucked.

Boom! Frenchy shot off the sofa arm, swatting the rubber band halfway across the room with her right paw.

I pulled a yellow one out of the packet and flung it high into the air, toward the center of the room. Frenchy watched it with enormous concentration. Just as it hit the floor, she pounced on it and started to roll over across the room, pummeling her new toy as she went.

Yes, my rubber bands were quite a success.

When she was tired of the game she returned to the sofa, where we had a conversation about loneliness and assorted matters.

I left the Woburn apartment and walked north on Broadway to deliver the tuna check as requested.

It took me a while to find Dino's. I had been looking for either a posh pet store or a gourmet shop. Instead, it turned out to be just a small, garden-variety bodega.

I walked inside. Shelves in the narrow aisles were very high and packed densely with canned goods. The store appeared empty except for the middle-aged man behind the counter clad in the generic white delicatessen apron.

"Hello," I said. "Beatrice Woburn asked me to deliver this." I handed the check across the counter.

He nodded, then signaled that I should hold on to it for a minute while he opened a small cardboard file box.

"She said you were to deliver it the day after tomorrow," I reminded him.

He nodded again, in a formal way, as if he were an apothecary in a small Midwestern town that didn't have to be reminded that Mrs. Jones needed her heart medicine delivered.

He riffled through the cards in the file box. Then his face seemed to relax. He had found the order.

Just as he was extracting the note or receipt or whatever it was from the box, I heard a sound behind me.

A sort of *click.*

But I didn't turn around then, for the aproned man behind the counter made a louder noise—a kind of expelling of breath, as if he had felt a sudden pain.

There was certainly no doubt that he had turned paste white.

Finally I did look over my shoulder. And then it was my turn to go pale.

Just inside the door, about five feet from the counter, stood a young man. He was dressed all in black. On his face was the most ridiculous mask—a kind of Lone Ranger thing painted silver.

Was there some kind of joke being played? How I wanted to believe that.

But no. This was no joke.

Both his hands were thrust toward us, and in them was a cocked 9 mm handgun.

He spoke in an extremely calm voice: "The man behind the counter must open the register, then open the drawer underneath the counter with the lottery ticket receipts; then move out from behind the counter and join the tall woman.''

That's what he said. The store owner did as he was told.

But as he was joining me, I heard another sound. A heavy thud.

We all turned toward it. A woman with several cans of Progresso split pea soup had just emerged from an aisle. I hadn't known anyone else was in the store. She had obviously turned the corner, seen the gunman, and startled, dropped part of her bundle.

The counterman raised his hand to calm her, moving in front of me.

''No!'' shouted the masked man.

The weapon jerked in his hand. The sound of his gun was like the bark of an angry dog.

The counterman fell, blood pumping out of the side of his head.

The shooter ran out.

The soup woman and I stared at each other in mute terror.

What she was thinking, I do not know. What flashed through my mind was precise: The gunman had been aiming at me.

The man down there, on the floor, had inadvertently saved me.

He died before the ambulance arrived.

Chapter 2

I didn't get back to my apartment until 9 P.M. The beasts were furious; where the hell was their evening meal?

Oh yes! How they wailed!

Bushy, my Maine coon, was high stepping in his fury. Pancho, my rather psychotic gray alley cat with only one-third of a tail, abandoned his dashes across the loft and just sat on his haunches staring at me—betrayed.

"Don't you understand?" I shouted at them, as I spooned their delicacies into their dishes. "A man was murdered! *I* was almost murdered!"

They didn't seem to believe my story. I sat down at my battered dining room table with a box of crackers and a glass of water. I was bone weary.

The other witness to the robbery and the murder, the soup can lady, had been sent home hours before. We had both told the same story.

And given the NYPD detectives the same description of the shooter, right down to the ridiculous Lone Ranger mask.

But one of the detectives, a pale, ferocious little woman named Sonia Little, did not believe me. She felt I was withholding something. And she was absolutely right.

Of course, what I was withholding was my belief that the bullet was meant for me.

Should I have told Detective Little? Probably.

Would it have mattered given their construction of a botched robbery scenario? I doubt it.

Would Detective Little have given any credence whatsoever to my story? Not in a million years. Why not? It was a classic response of a hysterical woman in shock, leavened by a dose of paranoia.

I chewed a cracker. I knew what I knew; I had been set up.

As crazy and as outlandish as it seemed, for some inexplicable reason, Beatrice Woburn wanted me dead. The note and the errand was a setup. The Lone Ranger was in her employ.

Ordinarily, I would have called Tony, or Nora, or Sam Tully. They were all inaccessible now.

What a time to be alone. The crackers started to taste like stale corn meal. I decided to wash them down with 2 percent milk instead of water—then I fell into bed.

The next morning, at eight-eleven, my aloneness vanished. Someone was leaning on the bell downstairs. I threw on a robe, buzzed the pilgrim in, and went into my standard security mode . . . going into the hall and standing at the top of the landing so I could see the intruder two landings down and verify whether it was a derelict, a meter reader, an enemy, or a friend. An intercom was obviously needed but not yet installed.

There were two people climbing the stairs. One of them as Elias Almodovar. Beside him was a tall young woman with wild blond hair and a bizarre makeup scheme including eye pencil that made her brows look like wings.

I was astonished and happy to see him. He paused about ten feet below me.

"I heard all about it this morning. Oh Alice! It must have been horrible." He pulled out a bouquet of yellow roses. "So I thought you could use a little company."

My eyes filled with tears. Say what you want about actors—but when bad things happen in the real world, they know how to be gallant.

I took them into my apartment and made them coffee. The young woman, whom he introduced as Terry Ray, was obviously his girlfriend. She had a slight Southern accent.

I put the roses in water and set them on a window ledge. They were brilliant in the morning light.

"Were you frightened, Alice?" he asked.

"During the holdup? Yes."

"And when he fired?"

"I think I just went into shock."

"In Houston, where I come from," Terry Ray said, "they hold up one bodega a day."

"He was going for the lottery receipts, I guess," said Elias.

I sat down and Terry leaned toward me. "Was he really wearing a Lone Ranger mask?"

"It sure looked like one."

Elias shook his head sadly. "I used to go into that bodega, Alice. Not often but once in a while. I remember that man behind the counter . . . the one who was shot. He never said much but he seemed to be a kind, gentle man. It's so sad."

And then Elias did a startling thing.

He slipped off the chair and kneeled on the floor, intoning:

" 'Therefore, you now have sorrow; but I will see you again and your heart will rejoice, and your joy no one will take from you.

" 'And in that day you will ask Me nothing.

Most assuredly, I say to you, whatever you ask the Father in My name He will give you.' "

Then he whispered, "John, Chapter 16, verses 22 and 23."

Terry Ray barked at him: "Please, Elias, get up! You're embarrassing me!

"Did you know that Elias is 'born again'?" she asked me.

I didn't, and I didn't know what to say. Elias got back onto the chair. His hands were still folded. I really wasn't that surprised. Out-of-work actors, no matter their age, develop a whole range of desperate behavior. Some do yoga, some shoplift, some try acupuncture, and some find God.

But the spontaneity of his kneeling on the floor seemed to empower me, to make me totally honest . . . to make me confess.

"Elias, I think I was set up."

"What do you mean?" He asked.

"I went to the bodega because Beatrice Woburn sent me there, to pay for some birthday cat food. I think she planned a fake holdup. I think she hired the shooter. I think it was I he aimed at."

Terry Ray laughed nervously: "Are you serious?"

Elias said nothing for the longest time. He seemed to be staring into his folded hands.

"Did you hear what I said, Elias?"

He nodded but was still silent. Finally, he slowly unfolded his hands as if it was painful for him to do so and said, "I hear it well."

"Do you think it's a fantasy, Elias? Do you think I am off the wall? Do you think I am constructing a role without a script?"

He shook his head. He stared at Terry, then at me. He picked his small handsome head up and smiled wanly, like old men smile.

"I have something to tell you, Alice," he said.

"She's probably already read the Gospel of John," Terry said, mockingly.

"It's about Beatrice Woburn," he continued, ignoring her.

"Yes?"

"Two weeks ago. Beatrice was visiting the cat. You were in the apartment. I was on duty. She came down. The cat had scratched her."

"Yes, yes, I remember. But it was nothing, a small scratch. Frenchy scratched me the same way."

"Mrs. Woburn started speaking to me, right there in the lobby, as if I was a friend of hers . . . a confidant. Which I surely wasn't." He was talking fast, almost babbling. "She made an accusation, Alice."

"A what?"

"An accusation—against you."

"An accusation of what?"

"She claimed you had turned the cat against her. She claimed there was a conspiracy against her mounted by you and her husband . . . to make Frenchy hate her . . . to take Frenchy away from her."

I laughed derisively.

"The woman is mad, Elias, mad as the proverbial hatter, and then some. Frenchy will scratch anyone who tries to pick her up from behind."

"I am just telling you what I heard."

I got up from the chair and visited the yellow roses. Then I walked back. Suddenly I was furious. "Can she possibly be that crazy? To try and kill me over a scratch?"

"I don't know," Elias replied.

"You people don't know how funny you sound. The conversation is absurd, if you will pardon me for saying so. You didn't get shot, Alice. And Elias is in a different dimension now that he's been born again. He sees conspiracies and crucifixions everywhere. What he needs is a steady gig in a Latino soap opera."

Terry Ray's caustic judgment aborted the conversation. They left five minutes later.

One thing was clear, I realized. I had to find out just how dangerous Beatrice Woburn was.

Chapter 3

How does one deal with . . . rein in . . . evaluate—a possible homicidal maniac?

Talk to her lawyer, if she has one. It wasn't as bizarre as it seemed . . . not in this case.

Who else was I supposed to talk to? Her soon-to-be ex-husband? Hardly. Her children? They didn't know me at all. Her hairdresser? I didn't know him or her.

But her attorney, A.G. Roth . . . him I had met . . . twice in fact.

It was during the negotiation and signing of the cat-sitting contract, in Paulus Darien's office. Darien, of course, represented the husband.

The ludicrous formality of signing a cat-sitting contract had embarrassed A.G. Roth; I could tell that, and his discomfort made him okay in my book.

There was another reason why I had to speak to Roth—to resign. Alas, Frenchy and I, as the saying goes, were history. I did love felines in general and Frenchy in particular, but I still had a healthy respect for my life and limbs.

So, three hours after Elias and his friend had left, I plucked A.G. Roth's business card from the shambles of my wallet and made the call.

He answered on the second ring, was extremely polite, voiced his horror and concern at the shooting, and said he would be delighted to see me.

"Now?" I pressed.

There was a pause. Then he said—sure. His business card had only fax and telephone numbers. I assumed he had a posh uptown office, like Darien's. But the address he gave me was on Twelfth Street and Fourth Avenue.

I arrived at around one-thirty. The address he gave me was an apartment building. That was odd. I walked in, stated my business to the doorman, and was directed to an eleventh-floor apartment, although the doorman did use the term "Suite" 1108.

He opened the door when I rang, and I walked inside. Immediately I realized that A.G. Roth practiced law out of his apartment.

He saw the look on my face and laughed.

"I guess, Miss Nestleton, you thought I was one of those high-powered, big-bucks divorce lawyers like Paulus Darien. By no means. In fact, I'm not a divorce lawyer at all. Beatrice should have hired one but she's stubborn. My field is the law of artistic properties . . . you know, contracts between artists and galleries, between artists and museums, between artists and you name it. I was making big bucks in the 1980s when the art market was on a roller coaster up. Now I'm just a little old ambulance chaser, because no matter what you read in the newspapers, the art world has never recovered."

He pointed to a leather chair in the living room. I sat down. He was a kindly-looking middle-aged man with thick brown gray hair that he wore just a little too long for his age. His face was handsome but a bit crushed, as if he had been a wrestler in college. He spoke very softly. He was wearing an ill-fitting suit and ill-matching tie—as if making fun of his own outfit. He had a strange kind of magnetism, like a well-fed prowling cat that was about to purr but never did.

He sat down across from me. "Have you recovered from your ordeal?"

"Yes, I think so."

"Would you like some coffee?"

"No thanks." I looked around the living room qua office. He had made absolutely no attempt to make it appear businesslike. In fact, the whole place was in a kind of muted chaos; like the living quarters of a book collector. There were stacks of books and periodicals everywhere. Actually, coffee would have been nice but I had the feeling his coffee would have been atrocious.

I got to the first of my points quickly.

"I want to be relieved of my contractual duties pertaining to Frenchy."

He seemed startled.

"Do you think there will be any problem about that, Mr. Roth?"

He recovered quickly. "You mean contractually? Oh, no, no! Forget the contract. It was absurd, for show, to make the parties in the divorce feel good. And given the circumstances—but look—perhaps if you take a rest and then come back . . . After all, the compensation is quite respectable."

"You don't understand. I won't cat-sit in a place where the owner of said cat is trying to murder me."

"Oh come now! Are you making a joke?"

There and then I told him exactly what I thought about his client Beatrice Woburn.

When I had finished he asked: "Do you like duck?"

"What?"

"There's a new Chinese restaurant on Fourth Avenue that has a wonderful lunch special: roast duck over white rice, and for starters, exceptional scallion pancakes. I'm hungry. Please join me."

It was an odd response to my charge, but yes, I would have some duck while waiting for a real explanation of some kind.

We went downstairs, walked two blocks, and entered a bright new restaurant. The tablecloths were crisp and white; the plates shimmering with Asian patterns. We both ordered the duck special.

"I understand you're an actress."

"Yes. Have you seen me work?"

"I don't get to the theater."

"Then you haven't . . . seen my work, that is."

"More's the pity. It's not that I dislike the theater. On the contrary. I love it. But for some odd reason I just never go. Of course, everyone has things they enjoy but don't participate in."

"Like alcohol?" I asked, bemused.

"For one. Or hiking. Or, well, a thousand things."

The pancakes came. He took a bite of one, then put it down. "Now," he said, "would you kindly give me some facts supporting your view that my client is a murderess."

"With pleasure," I retorted.

Then I gave him a blow-by-blow account of the bodega tragedy. And a verbatim record of

Elias's reportage on the conspiratorial cat scratch as told him by Beatrice Woburn.

As I talked, A.G. Roth played with the scallion pancake.

When I had finished, he took another bite and noted: "An interesting tale. From a legal point of view, meaningless, of course. You really don't have one shred of evidence that the bullet was meant for you. And the conversation between Beatrice and the doorman concerning a conspiracy to turn Frenchy against her—well, it doesn't sound to me like Beatrice talking, and since you don't have a verbatim record—tape or otherwise—I'm skeptical in the extreme."

He stared at me harshly for a second or so and then continued. "Besides, what do you expect me to do about your beliefs, or your feelings, or whatever?"

"I don't know."

"You could tell the police."

"They'd laugh."

"That's true."

We seemed to be suspended somewhere—just sitting there in silence, but I didn't feel uncomfortable. The main dishes came. The duck was delicious. The rice was just the way I liked it—a bit cool, a bit wet, a bit salty. From time to time I stole a glance at A.G. Roth.

Clearly, he hadn't believed a word I said. But

he didn't seem to think I was a paranoid hysteric. He ate calmly, as if these kinds of accusations against his client were quite common.

Then, out of the blue came: "Miss Nestleton, were you ever divorced?"

"Married once, divorced once—a long time ago."

"I've never been married or divorced. But all my friends and colleagues have been. And I've observed something. There is a certain level at which a divorce turns from neutrality and relief into something ugly. When it crosses over that line, the participants begin to lose their bearings. They may become depressed or violent or slovenly or overfastidious or vengeful. Whatever—they change their character . . . the bumps in the nights begin to appear. Do you think this is a fair statement, Miss Nestleton?"

"Yes, of course."

"Well, that happened to Beatrice Woburn. But she didn't really become conspiratorial and homicidal, as you suggest. Believe me, she is incapable of that. All she became is eccentric . . . an eccentric middle-aged lady who is turning in circles."

"In other words, Mr. Roth, you think I'm just whistling Dixie."

"Yes."

"In other words, you think I'm a fool."

"No. On the contrary, I think you're a beautiful, wise woman with just a little bit too much of a theatrical sensibility."

I glared at him.

Then he did a very peculiar thing. He reached over the table with his right hand and covered my left hand.

He said: "Why don't you come back to my apartment now?"

I stared at his hand. I smiled.

"You know," I said, "it has been a long time since I received such a crude sexual proposition."

He pulled his hand away quickly.

"I assume the check is yours," I said bitterly, and walked out.

I was fuming. I headed uptown and didn't calm down until I found myself in Union Square Park. The afternoon was mild, mind-boggling in its beauty. A classical June day in New York City—zephyrs abounding.

Suddenly I realized that it was the first time I had been in that park in years. How things had changed! In the 1970s, when I moved to New York, it was a place to be avoided, filled with junkies, derelicts, and recently released mental patients.

Now there was grass and students and baby

carriages and people laughing and lovers lolling on the lawns. The change was dazzling.

I sat down on a bench and composed myself. I thought of Frenchy. Why, I don't know. I thought how nice it would be to take Frenchy out of that apartment for a while and let her gambol—if that was her preference.

But I would not be seeing Frenchy again—would I? And apartment cats rarely like the great outdoors unless they have a healthy dose of alley cat in them.

I rested on that bench for a few hours; then headed west on Fourteenth Street. And walked all the way home, slowly, window-shopping with a vengeance.

There was a phone message waiting for me, from, of all people, Beatrice Woburn's husband, Sidney. I had met him briefly, only once, during a visit to the quarantined apartment to socialize with Frenchy. He didn't come as often as his wife.

The message was simple and rather arrogant. I should be in his office in the morning at ten.

What in heaven's name could that man want?

Two rather chilling thoughts occurred to me. He was going to proposition me, sexually, like A.G. Roth. Really, I was a bit old for this kind of nonsense.

Or he was going to attempt to murder me, like his wife had. The Lone Ranger rides again.

I was too tired to worry about it. I fed the cats, listened to WKCR on the radio, and went to sleep very early. Bushy for some reason decided to take my pillow.

Chapter 4

Sidney Woburn owned an ugly five-story building as far west on Twenty-seventh Street as one could go without falling off the island.

The building was filled with computers, machines with huge screens that seemed halfway between computers and printing presses, and many other mysterious objects. Woburn's graphic arts firm produced everything from fashion magazines to car decals.

He was waiting for me in his office, which really wasn't an office at all, but a storeroom with a long steel table on which was a beat-up phone and a fax machine, along with two boxes of tissues.

Along the walls were huge rolls and containers of I knew not what. There were no chairs in this office. I stood on one side of the table and Sidney Woburn stood on the other side. He was a wiry bald man with thick glasses. All his movements and speech were abrupt and agitated. He was wearing an open sports shirt, brightly patterned. His upper body was twisted a bit, from age and arthritis no doubt.

"You well?" he asked.

"More or less."

"Good. Things happen. People die. Cities blow up. Buildings collapse. Tornadoes. Earthquakes. Guns. Plagues."

He walked to the window. Then he walked back to the table. "You get my drift?"

I burst out laughing.

"What's so funny?"

I couldn't tell him that "Get my drift?" was a phrase my derelict friend Sam Tully always used. It was so archaic . . . what drift?

"I wasn't laughing at you, Mr. Woburn. It's just I haven't the faintest notion what you're talking about."

He glared at me over his glasses.

"What I'm talking about is Frenchy. She needs you."

How stupid I had been! I should have realized that A.G. Roth would have told the other lawyer about my resignation; and Darien no doubt had told his client, Sidney Woburn. This trip was totally unnecessary.

"My mind is made up, Mr. Woburn. I am no longer Frenchy's cat-sitter."

"What if we sweeten the pot?"

I smiled. Obviously, A.G. Roth had not disclosed the reason for my resignation. That was good.

"No. The pay was more than generous. It's not the money."

"This is terrible!"

"No it isn't. Believe me, you'll have no trouble finding a competent sitter for Frenchy, none at all."

The phone rang then. It was more a groan from the old battered phone. There was no answering machine attached. Sidney stared at the phone. It kept on ringing. He still didn't pick up. He looked at me and said, "That's either my lawyer or my daughter." He said it in a way that meant he didn't want to hear from either of them.

Finally, he picked up. He didn't say a word. He just listened for a minute, then said, "Okay," and finally hung up.

"It was Rachel, my daughter. She needs money. But she always needs money. We bought her the co-op and she still can't make the monthly maintenance. That's the way it is with actresses. Right, Miss Nestleton? You can sit for the rent. Rachel does nothing but pick up the phone. Actually, she doesn't like being called an actress. Comedienne, or performer, or performance artist. That's what she wants to be called. Can you imagine that?"

He took out his wallet and peered inside to check his cash situation.

"You live on the Lower West Side, don't you, Miss Nestleton?"

"Yes."

"Well, Rachel lives on Twenty-first between Ninth and Tenth. I'll drop you off there."

"That will be fine."

We exited the building together and headed for the corner to get a cab. He stopped suddenly. "Would you do me a favor?"

"If it's not a cat-sitting favor," I replied, a bit testily.

"Rachel and I really don't get along. Would you come up to her apartment with me? There's never a fight if a third party is in attendance. Sort of insurance. It'll only be a few minutes; then I'll take you right to your door."

How could I refuse a father's plea?

Rachel Woburn lived in a very old row house—on the top floor. The apartment itself—structurally—was breathtaking. The space was small, the hallways narrow, but the ceilings were extremely high and every room had its own skylight.

The moment we entered, the rusty-haired

young woman called out in a mocking tone: "Daddy dear, daddy dear. You of the fat heart."

I froze in a kind of horror when I heard those words; they were a paraphrase of some lines from a very nasty Sylvia Plath poem written to the father she loathed.

"This is Alice Nestleton," Sidney announced.

"Ah, the famous cat-sitter. Enter. Enter. My father brings me money. My mother brings me art. Maybe you bring hope."

"I doubt that," I muttered.

She led us into the kitchen. Sidney sat down. I sat down. Rachel poured us apple juice in coffee cups.

"The cash, Daddy, the cash."

Her father took out his wallet and counted out a few hundred dollars in twenties and fifties. Then he wrote her a check.

The situation was so uncomfortable I searched desperately for an alternative focus. And I found one, on the wall, right above me. There hung the largest green canvas pot holder I have ever seen.

It took me a while to realize it wasn't a functional thing . . . it was, in fact, a rather stunning work of art . . . and it had a shape over and above the pot holder. It was a tortoise, and it was woven rather than canvas, and done in the Navajo fashion, tongue in cheek. I realized I was looking at one of Beatrice Woburn's textile pieces.

The financial transaction completed, father and daughter sat stiffly, not knowing what to say. I was no help.

We left two minutes later. Sidney Woburn dropped me off in a cab on Hudson Street, a block from my place. He was so depressed he didn't say another word.

As I turned my key in the outside lock, I heard: "Miss Nestleton!"

I turned. Two women were standing by the curb in front of a car. One of them was the skeptical homicide detective, Sofia Little. The other woman was oddly familiar but I couldn't really place her.

Detective Little smiled a bit wickedly and asked, "Don't you remember Joan Wright?"

Ah, the lady with the soup cans in the bodega.

"Yes, yes," I said.

"We have good news," the detective announced. "The Lone Ranger has fallen off his horse."

Chapter 5

I sat in the backseat of the unmarked vehicle as Detective Little drove us to the precinct. I was, to say the least, a bit stunned.

"Well, not really fell off. Let's just say he rode his great white horse Silver right through a stop sign." Detective Little chuckled, explaining as she drove us to the lineup. "A traffic cop pulls him over in Queens and asks for registration. The fool opens his glove compartment and a mask falls out. Worse, a weapon is clearly visible. The cop makes the arrest. It turns out our hero has held up five stores in three states over the past three weeks. He's a very nervous Lone Ranger. The tally is three wounded and one dead. In fact, a few papers started calling him Nervous Nellie. Witnesses say he isn't savage, just nervous. Someone makes a move and *boom, boom!* He shoots."

Right then, I realized my whole case had collapsed.

My sureness dissolved.

My charges against Beatrice Woburn revealed themselves as absurd and pathetic.

My self-esteem took a nosedive—maybe I had been a hysterical paranoid. Of course I had, no maybes at all.

There were eight young men in the lineup.

I tentatively identified number three as the gunman. His face of course, in the bodega, had been masked. I made the ID from body shape and size. I was not absolutely sure, not at all.

Joan Wright was much more certain, indeed, emphatic. She stated that number three was the Lone Ranger.

All Detective Little said was "Good work. Thank you. He's the one. We're waiting for ballistics now."

Joan Wright and I stared at each other. It was odd why there was no friendship or intimacy between us—after all, we had shared the most dangerous of moments. But there was none. In fact, we seemed to make each other uncomfortable. Detective Little drove me home.

I walked upstairs in a fog. I had lost—thrown away—a lucrative cat-sitting job for no reason at all, and made a complete fool of myself in the bargain.

What I needed, I realized, was a long vacation, maybe a health spa in Switzerland where they would put me to sleep for a week or so and, in some mysterious way, rejuvenate mind, body, and soul.

I lay down and took a nap. When I woke up, I realized the Swiss spa idea would have to be shelved for financial reasons. It was growing dark. Oh, it was going to be a long, difficult night. The nap had guaranteed that I wouldn't sleep easily. And if I didn't sleep, there would be visions of shame dancing in my head. Hysterical actress. Frenchy, yawning and accusing. The Lone Ranger. Was I Tonto?

Emergency measures were needed. I broke out the vacuum cleaner—my cats' worst enemy. They wailed and fled. I had no mercy. I turned the monster on and vacuumed the entire loft. Then I scrubbed what passes for my kitchen. Then I polished my grandmother's silverware—what I had left of it. Then I stacked and tied newspapers; searched for holes in stockings, socks, and panty hose; prepared a respectable laundry; made out the shopping lists; and broke one cup while cleaning shelves.

Around midnight I collapsed.

The next morning I stopped feeling sorry for myself, did intelligent chores, contacted my agent, and started looking for new cat-sitting jobs.

My new life was interrupted by A.G. Roth. He called around noon.

"First," he said, "I wish to apologize for my crudeness."

"Okay," I replied. For some strange reason I was happy to hear his voice. And before he could say another word, I blurted out, "By the way, everything I told you about Beatrice Woburn has turned out to be untrue."

"I couldn't care less," he replied.

"Well, I just wanted to set the record straight."

Bushy, I noted, was now staring at the phone. But that was not unusual; he had a thing with phone voices. I believe he considered them mice about to emerge, and this excited him, predator that he was.

"Do you accept my apology?"

"Yes, of course."

"Good. Then you'll have dinner with me tonight."

"I'm afraid not."

"I thought we could try for an off-Broadway play afterwards, or a movie."

"No thank you."

"Then you don't forgive me."

"Didn't you hear me, Mr. Roth? I do forgive you. But I don't want to have dinner with you."

"That grieves me," he said.

I burst out laughing. He sounded pathetic. It was cruel to laugh. He thanked me and hung up the phone. I didn't know what to do. I felt stupid. What could I have done? Gone to dinner with him? No. But I should have been more civil. The man disturbed me in some manner. I didn't know how or why.

I headed out to perform my shopping lists.

To my astonishment, there was Detective Sofia Little again, lounging in front of her vehicle.

"I was just about to ring your bell," she said.

"Something go wrong with the ID?" I asked.

"No. Do you know a man named Elias Almodovar?"

"Yes. Of course. An actor. He's a substitute doorman where I cat-sit."

"Can I see your driver's license?"

"What?"

"Your driver's license. You do have one, don't you?"

"Sure. But what's this about?"

"Your driver's license, please," she repeated, this time with a very hard edge.

I opened my wallet and dug out my license.

I handed it to her. She studied it for a while, then handed it back.

"Thank you," she said. "Elias Almodovar died early this morning from stab wounds inflicted when he fought back during an attempted robbery of his person, on the street, only three blocks from where he worked."

I was horrified, confused. I didn't say a word.

"The assailants fled without getting anything."

She pulled something out of her pocket and handed it to me, saying, "This was in his wallet."

It was a driver's license. And it had my photo on it. It was *my* license. But how could that be? I had just put mine back into my wallet.

"I don't understand," I said unhappily.

"Neither do I. Are you sure you can't give me an explanation, Miss Nestleton?"

"I just showed you my license. How can there be two of them?"

She took the object back.

"Were you and this Almodovar close?" she asked.

"No. I hadn't seen him for years when I bumped into him. We would talk and reminisce at the building. He came to see me after the bodega shooting, with his girlfriend."

"That would be Terry Ray?"

"Yes."

"And you never gave him your license to reproduce?"

"Of course not."

She stared at me. I was becoming agitated. It was bad enough that Elias had been murdered. But this license thing seemed to verge on the occult, on witchcraft, on voodoo, as if I was being hunted by unseen forces, as if there were a netherworld I was participating in without my conscious knowledge. How many Alice Nestleton New York State driver's licenses were in existence? How many Alice Nestletons were there in existence?

"If you remember anything further about your relationship with this Almodovar, Miss Nestleton, please call me immediately. I assume there is a lot you have not told me." And with that rather tart comment, Detective Little ambled off.

I aborted my shopping journey, went right back upstairs, and sat down on my one easy chair. I felt exhausted, drained, lifeless.

Elias had been with me, right here in my loft, twenty-four hours ago. Or was it forty-eight? What did it matter?

How did my driver's license get into his wallet? Or rather, a knockoff of my license.

Think, Alice, think.

I stared at the yellow roses he had brought me. They were fading fast.

There was, I realized, one possibility and one only. When I had first started to cat-sit Frenchy and bumped into Elias after all those years, he had come up to visit me a few times. It was always on his lunch hour. We would reminisce happily but he never stayed long. We just sat around and talked about old theater friends and productions.

He could have, without my seeing, when I was busy with Frenchy, removed my driver's license from my wallet, brought it to a photostat source, and then returned the original during the next visit. This was possible—barely.

But there was one huge problem with my speculation. Elias was "born again." I had seen him with my own eyes, dropping down on the floor to pray. "Born again" people tend not to be thieves—maybe before the experience but surely not after it.

Besides, what possible use could my driver's license be to him?

It was getting crazy. Why was I obsessing about the stupid license? The poor man had been butchered.

Oh, I was in bad shape. I had to speak to someone. But who? Sam Tully? Yes, he was the only game in town.

I picked up the phone. No! I slammed it down. I'll just go right over. I knew where he was and what he was doing . . . in his apartment, typing, trying to turn his old hard-boiled detective Harry Bondo, the star of that out-of-print mystery series, into a kinder, gentler sleuth. And thereby get the series resurrected.

I walked fast the six blocks to his Spring Street apartment and leaned on the downstairs buzzer. A return ring. Good. He was in, as I had suspected.

I ran up the stairs. He was standing in the doorway.

"Figured it might be you. Who else could it be?"

I could not believe he was wearing a winter coat . . . an overcoat.

"Sam, it's June."

"Yeah. But I'm hot on the keys if you know what I mean. So I put my good luck overcoat on to make sure the juices keep flowing."

He looked terrible, as usual, like a cherubic derelict who had just been released from a hospital. His frizzled hair and beard were matted. Underneath the overcoat he wore a tattered pair of khaki pants and a faded T-shirt with the advertising logo of an auto repair business uptown.

I walked inside, almost choking on the cigarette smoke, even though the windows were wide open. His cat Pickles was outside on the fire escape, staring in—his strange spotted coat, like a leopard's, reflecting the sun. Pickles always moved freely up and down the fire escape, from roof to apartment, and Sam did absolutely nothing to restrain him.

"You're just in time for a late lunch," he said, pointing to a small folding table set up next to his desk, chair, and typewriter. On the table was a carton of buttermilk, a packet of processed American cheese, and two very plain and very stale bagels. There was also an open can of what seemed to be anchovies. It was enough to induce instant nausea. I declined with thanks.

"I'm going to send you pages soon, Nestleton. I want your input," Sam said, sitting down and starting to pound maniacally on the ancient machine.

"I'd be delighted to read them," I said.

"I think you'll love it. I got Harry Bondo quoting Byron and Shelley as he takes apart two hoods." He chuckled and pounded harder. "Talk, honey. I'm listening."

I told him about the bodega shooting.

He laughed and said: "The fact is, Nestleton, where you go, trouble shows up."

Then I told him about the death of my friend

Elias and the mysterious duplicate of my driver's license that was found among his possessions.

He laughed even harder and said: "I once had a girlfriend who stole my license, my credit cards, my silk handkerchiefs, and my apartment lease."

It was obvious our conversation was going nowhere. It was obvious he was not able to provide me with the support I needed. I walked to the window and reached out to Pickles. The cat hissed, crouched, and laid his ears back.

It was no use at all. I said goodbye and walked downstairs. I stood on Spring Street, most unhappy. I didn't want to go home. I wanted . . . I don't know what I wanted.

But I know what I did. I walked to the pay phone and called A.G. Roth.

I told him I didn't want dinner. I didn't want an off-Broadway play or a movie. What I wanted was some food now. Was he available?

"Where are you?" he asked simply.

I told him.

He said, "Stay right there."

Thirty minutes later we were sitting in a posh new French restaurant called Balthazar on Spring Street, a few blocks east of Sam's apartment.

The moment we sat down in the booth, he asked, "Why did you change your mind?"

What could I tell him? That I was lonely and confused and just needed a shoulder? No. That my friends were all out of town or busy? No.

"Pique," I replied.

"Is that a sauce?" he asked, smiling.

"No. But at these prices maybe that's all we should order."

"I always order a hamburger in a French restaurant. It makes the waiter think I'm too hip to mess around with," he noted.

So that's what we both did—order hamburgers, green salad, and red wine.

Actually, the place where we were sitting, the booth area, away from the large dining room, was quite nice. The main lunch crowd was gone but there were still enough for a loud buzz—and there was a constant friendly click and clank of dishes and trays.

"As for what happened in that Chinese restaurant . . . I just don't know . . . I was mortified after I realized what I had done. Believe me, I am somewhat shy . . . I don't go around propositioning women, no matter how beautiful or desirable they are." He spoke the words very quickly and very quietly, into his salad.

I laughed. "So that is what I am, huh? Beautiful and desirable. My, my. I always thought I was just a little farm girl . . . too tall to hide in the corn and too old now to harvest it."

Suddenly I was feeling much better . . . more in control. The restaurant soothed me and so, in a way, did A.G. Roth. I stopped obsessing about Elias and the licenses. They just slipped out of my mind . . . out of range . . . out of focus.

Was it the red wine?

The eleven-dollar hamburgers arrived. Actually they were ten ninety-five each. They were delicious.

"What does A.G. stand for?" I asked.

"You mean—what do people call me?"

"Okay."

"A.G."

I smiled at him. There was something a bit off-kilter with this man, but in a nice way.

"And what do they call you?" he asked.

"Alice."

"Is it a stage name?"

"No. A Minnesota name."

"So that's where you're from?"

I nodded. "And where are you from, A.G.?"

"Originally, Brooklyn."

"Is that in the Netherlands?"

We both laughed and drank more wine.

"Do you take clients to this place?" I queried.

"I don't take clients anywhere. I fact, I don't have too many clients left."

"You don't sound happy about the way you make a living."

"I'm not. I didn't really want to be a lawyer."

"What did you want to be?"

"A criminologist."

"Are you serious?"

"Quite serious."

And then he gave me a hurt look. I got just a bit nervous. Did he know something about me? Was this some kind of setup? Did he know I had participated in several criminal investigations? Did he know that certain elements of the NYPD had, in the past, called me The Cat Woman? It was hard to tell.

I had to play it by ear.

"You ought to meet a friend of mine, then. His name is Sam Tully. He writes mystery novels. He created a famous hard-boiled detective named Harry Bondo."

He raised his eyebrows.

"I'm not talking about Hollywood pulp fantasies," he replied in an insulted tone. "When I say criminology, I mean something like . . . well . . . for example . . . Lincoln."

"Ah, you mean the Lincoln assassination."

"Yes."

"Then you're one of those conspiracy buffs."

"Please, you're insulting me again. Those people are fools. I'm talking about a quiet, scholarly, logical, retrospective investigation into all the events leading to the murder of Lincoln and the so-called denouement of the case. And Napoleon for that matter. Even Alexander the Great."

"I thought Napoleon died a natural death on that island."

"Many people do. In my opinion, they're wrong. In my opinion, he was murdered by the administration of poison by person or persons associated with his physician."

We ordered brandy, coffee, and a single tart to split. My my, I thought, this conversation is moving into uncharted waters.

"Do you often indulge in this hobby, A.G.?" I asked. It was fun speaking his initials.

"Not a hobby. Don't call it a hobby. It's a passion. It's in my head all the time. What little money I make, after expenses, goes to feed the passion."

"Which is why you have no office."

"Probably."

"What was your most recent feeding of this passion?"

"Aah," he exhaled, sipped his brandy and almost purred: "From London."

"Jack the Ripper memorabilia?" I chided him. The wine was definitely going to my head.

"No. A sheaf of drawings that were reproduced in London newspapers the week after the assassination of Lincoln. They accompanied the reportage and they were attempts to provide a detailed construction of the scene of the crime and the milieu."

"They sound fascinating."

"They're astonishing. I'd love to show them to you, but I know if I asked you to come up to my apartment, you'd think I was making another crude pass . . . like the proverbial artist who asks the proverbial woman to come up and see his proverbial etchings. I am assuming that you view me as a man just chock-full of nefarious sexual propositions."

"On the contrary, A.G. Of the men I have been meeting recently, you are among the least nefarious."

So, after the desert, I went up to his apartment with him.

It was a bad mistake.

Oh, the sheaf of drawings was fascinating.

But five minutes after perusing the pictures, we were in each other's arms.

And five minutes later we were in bed.

I have no idea why it happened so fast like that.

I didn't leave the apartment until midnight. He said to me as I left: "I hope you understand. I am, within the limits of my age and sensibility, totally, head-over-heels in love with you and I have been from the first moment I saw you in Darien's office."

Chapter 6

When I woke up the next morning at the startlingly late hour of nine, I felt so strange and probably looked so strange that there was not a single wail from my kitties for their overdue breakfast. They just prowled alongside the bed, back and forth, making those pathetic little mews in their stomach like they were being beaten and were too brave to really howl.

I did get up and feed them but I was walking strangely, a bit zombie-like.

The coffee I made was bitter. I sipped it slowly and in the fullness of the morning light tried to figure out exactly what the hell had happened.

Look—my relationship with Tony Basillio was long-standing, but always precarious.

He had never really been faithful to me; his obsession with young actresses was often overwhelming.

I had been a lot more faithful, but not totally. Over the years I had had affairs. A few. They were short-lived . . . and they were not satisfying except for the illicit frisson.

But what happened to me last night was different.

In the past, the few times I had strayed, I had done it carefully . . . plotting and reasoning it out.

I stalked the gentleman or let myself be stalked.

This thing with A.G. Roth had just happened, erupted, exploded. It seemed to be random . . . worse . . . it seemed to be promiscuous. That is a word I fear and loathe.

Of course there were circumstances.

I was lonely.

Several bad things had occurred and made me shaky.

And in so many ways, the man had flattered me . . . had raised my self-esteem . . . had given me the sense that I was twenty-five again.

Or maybe it was just the ten ninety-five hamburger.

The phone rang. I let the answering machine handle it. I listened.

"Alice, this is Laura Arroyo. I hope you remember me. We worked together in 1981 or '82, at the New Playwrights' Group. I'm calling all

Elias's old friends. He'll be buried out in Jersey but there's a funeral service and viewing tomorrow at Kristle's on First Avenue between Ninety-fourth and Ninety-fifth Streets. Ten A.M. I hope you can make it. Oh, this is all so sad . . . so horrible. Poor Elias. He never could get a break . . . could he?"

And then she hung up. I didn't remember her. I didn't even remember the New Playwrights' Group. But yes, I would go.

I finished my coffee, showered and dressed. It was warm. I opened all the windows wide. From the top, of course.

The phone rang again.

Again I listened to the machine intercept and project the voice. It was A.G. Roth.

"I have two things to say. One: I haven't felt this good since I was in summer camp when I was eleven years old and I found a baby snapping turtle in one of my sneakers. Two: Meet me at Balthazar at six and we'll graduate to steak frites."

This man, I thought, even though gentle, seems to have a red meat addiction. Not good.

I had to think this out now. I had to be calm, to make a decision. Read a little, I thought. Get your brain cells working.

The unread books on my shelf were daunting—novels, biographies, plays, memoirs. As of late, I rarely read, though I kept buying books even when I couldn't afford to.

My eyes fell on *Roseanna.* I smiled. The Swedish mystery writing team of Maj Sjöwall and Per Wahlöö had become a severe addiction for me when their books first started appearing in English in the 1970s. I read all of them. Alas, Wahlöö had died and the books came to a halt.

Roseanna had been one of my favorites.

Inspector Beck (his first name is Martin) solves a grisly murder of an American tourist whose badly decomposed body has been inadvertently dredged out of a canal. It requires a long, brilliant, two-continent investigation.

Yes, it would be nice to read *Roseanna* again. Inspector Beck was methodical and ruthlessly deductive. Surely this thing with A.G. Roth—whatever it was—needed some of that.

I plucked the old paperback from the shelf and propped myself up in the reading position on the bed, with an apple. I opened the book and went directly into another time, another place, another horror.

As strange as it may seem, I read that bloody book from cover to cover, in three hours, without moving, without ever taking a bite of the apple. I read fast, voraciously, like an adolescent. Some of it I remembered, and some of it I didn't.

When I was finished, I felt a bit drained, as I always do when I read a good book. I placed it reverentially back onto the shelf and took a long walk into Tribeca, stopping at the flower beds of the World Financial Center and then walking to the Hudson River, where I stared for a long time into the churning muddy water, like some German romantic poet.

I was back in the loft by three. There was no way, I realized, I would not be at Balthazar at six.

But I did dress down. Very much down. Almost poor. A kind of feminist *réssentiment*, perhaps, at being told by a man, any man, Meet me at . . .

A.G. Roth was already in the booth when I entered. There was no awkwardness or discomfort of any kind. Neither of us spoke. Our hands simply met across the table and held. The waitress, who was already on her way to serve us, seemed a bit embarrassed.

Believe me, I had no idea what was going on with this man and me.

He ordered steak frites. I ordered a vegetable tart. He chose the bottle of red wine. After that initial joining of hands, there was no further demonstration of affection. He asked me how I had spent the day. I told him about the mystery novel and my walk. He told me he had delivered some papers to Beatrice Woburn. Until the divorce was final, she was staying with a sister on the Upper East Side.

Then A.G. smiled at me. "Beatrice told me that Frenchy misses you."

"Believe me," I replied, "the missing is mutual. Frenchy is a lovely cat."

"You really don't like her, do you?"

"What are you talking about? I love Frenchy."

"No, Alice. I'm talking about Bea."

"I already apologized to you for suspecting her in that bodega shooting."

"I know, but you don't like her."

"I don't really know her."

"You have to understand that her situation is very sad, Alice. It's an ugly divorce. She's separated from her cat. She has an out-of-work actress of a daughter named Rachel who hates her. She has a son named Anton who's doing quite well but never contacts her. And a big textile art show she put together got burned out a day before it was supposed to open. And—"

"Wait, A.G.! Okay. I give up. I love your client now."

He laughed. We toasted Beatrice. We ate. We drank. He drank a lot. We ate outrageous desserts.

Then we went to his apartment, and believe it or not, we danced to rock and roll music.

Then he drank some more, not wine this time, and pushed me gently onto the sofa.

"Do you want to laugh?" he asked.

"I always want to laugh," I replied.

"Good. Remember I told you about Bea's out-of-work daughter, Rachel. Well, she's a very funny young lady. And I got a video of one of her comedic performances."

It dawned on me that I had never told A.G. that I had met Rachel.

"Do you really want to laugh?"

"I told you I did."

He went to a stack of videos and shuffled through them. Then he raised one high in triumph. "I got it. This is one she did as part of a comedy team. Believe me, they are funny."

He shoved it into the VCR. It took him a while to get it operating. Once the screen lit up, he tipsily flopped down beside me.

"Believe me, Alice Nestleton, you are going to laugh!"

It was a skit. Two young women in a luncheonette after a night of partying.

I recognized Rachel immediately.

The trouble was—I recognized the other woman also.

I jumped up and approached the screen to get a better look.

Then I shut it off.

"What are you doing? Give her a chance. She's funny."

"Her partner," I said, "is Terry Ray."

"Who's Terry Ray?"

"Elias's girl friend."

"Who's Elias?"

"An actor and a substitute doorman in your client's building. He was murdered the other day during a mugging."

A.G. looked totally confused.

"Don't you understand what a strange coincidence this is?"

"No."

"Building. Doorman. Girlfriend. Daughter. Me. The Woburn family." I realized I had just ticked off a sequence of names and persons in no particular order. Obviously, the sight of Terry Ray on the video had truly disturbed me.

"Relax, Alice, sit down. Don't worry about coincidence. It's always fool's gold. As I told you . . . deep down I'm a world-class criminologist." He paused, wobbling a bit. A.G. really had had too much to drink. So had I. He kissed me on the forehead. He continued his thought. "As I said, I have always found that coincidences are meaningless, worthless as a category. They are neither animal, vegetable, nor mineral. And unlike bread, they cannot be eaten, kneaded, baked, or . . ." He laughed and tried to kiss me with more intensity.

But suddenly I was not interested. He looked at me in shock for pulling away.

"Something is wrong," I muttered.

"With us?"

"No, A.G. No. I mean with the . . . world."

I left his apartment immediately. I had the strange feeling that something was . . . how shall I put it . . . perking somewhere . . . that a coffeepot was perking somewhere . . . that it was about to boil over . . . that the coffee would be ruined and a whole lot more. Yes, it was a very strange percolator fantasy.

And it truly frightened me.

Chapter 7

I left the loft at eight o'clock in the morning, took the M8 bus crosstown to First Avenue, and transferred to the uptown bus. I was dressed in what could be considered my June funeral best—a dark brown skirt and jacket, with a light brown blouse. I even wore a hat.

What a miserable night it had been. After I had walked out of A.G.'s place for no reason at all—what had he done?—I went home and brooded and obsessed over the coincidence.

I could not shake the belief that the fact that Terry Ray had once been a partner in comedy with Rachel Woburn was pregnant with threat and conspiracy.

It did lead me to the belief, though it was obviously not a logical progression, that the death of Elias Almodovar had not been what the police believed.

Just as the death of that counterman in the bodega had not been what I had believed.

And the center, the core of my disquiet, was the "born again" angle.

The police had characterized Elias's death as a botched mugging . . . just as they had characterized the bodega killing as a botched holdup. Obviously they were right in the latter.

But the coincidence of Terry and Rachel for some reason set me thinking: Elias would not have fought back against muggers.

Not because he was cowardly . . . but because he was "born again."

It was the same reason why I couldn't believe he had stolen my driver's license to knock off.

Was I giving too much credit to those who possessed devoutness? Particularly those who had achieved it dramatically . . . who had . . . like Elias . . . been "born again"?

Maybe.

As for the connection between Terry and Rachel Woburn: Why did it disturb me so much? I no longer thought a Woburn was out to murder me. My connection with all of them was severed, even with Frenchy.

As for A.G. Roth: Would I see him again? Didn't I want to see him again? Was I in love? Wasn't I in love? Wasn't it stupid for a woman of my age and my position, whatever that position was, to carry on like that? And what about Tony? What, indeed, about Tony!

The rush-hour uptown bus emptied most of its passengers by the time it reached Sixtieth Street. It was a leisurely ride for the next thirty blocks.

The funeral home was right on the street—a storefront—and seemed to be small, but once I was inside, it turned out to be a twisting series of warrens, with several funerals going on at once.

The Elias Almodovar affair was on the second floor. The body was laid out properly. Elias was in a suit he probably never wore while he was alive. He may have been born again, but now clearly he was dead forever.

There were only about ten people in the small chapel when I arrived.

I stared at his face; what a handsome man he was—so thin, so chiseled, almost beatific.

What had my grandmother once told me? Keep the coffin closed, Alice. Remember that. Keep the coffin closed.

Something rustled across the coffin—like a breeze. It frightened me. I stepped back.

"Search and ye shall find."

I turned to the voice and got more frightened. It was Terry Ray who had spoken. She was staring straight at me. Her eye makeup was even more garish than the last time I had seen her.

And she was wearing the most inappropriate funeral dress I had ever seen—orange taffeta, large billowy sleeves, and a Carmen Miranda hat.

She smiled at me.

I responded: "Seek what? Find what?"

"Did you love Elias?" she asked.

Her voice was clipped. The Houston accent had vanished completely. She looked older now than that time in my loft.

"In my fashion," I replied.

"Everyone does everything in their fucking fashion," she barked.

I was appalled by her language. This was a funeral.

And then her gaze, her whole person, oddly softened, and for a moment, for just a brief moment, there was a kind of intimate communion between us . . . as if we shared something about Elias.

She walked away. I was, as the expression goes, all shook up. The woman disturbed me. The woman made me suspicious. The woman was a cross to bear.

More people had entered the chapel, making it a respectable entourage. I saw faces from the past, old acting faces, without names. I nodded to them. They nodded to me.

I slid into a row of seats, sat down, and listened to the service. But I really wasn't hearing a word.

Why?

Because the situation had been clarified for me . . . purified . . . boiled down to its essence.

For a whole bundle of circumstantial, elliptical, allegorical, perhaps even outrageous and irrational reasons, including quirks within my own psyche . . . I believed that Elias Almodovar was murdered by persons associated with and controlled by Terry Ray.

When the service was over, the body was removed in its coffin . . . carried to the waiting hearse. I didn't stir. Soon the room was empty except for myself and a heavyset woman with a blue scarf on her head who sat at the end of my row.

I looked at her. She smiled and said, "I refuse to go to cemeteries anymore. I just refuse."

"You're Laura Arroyo, aren't you?" I said.

"Yes. Now do you remember me?"

"Of course. Thanks for calling me."

I really did remember her now. But she had changed dramatically—about forty pounds' worth.

"Are you still in the theater?" I asked.

"No. Not for years. I own a small office temp agency."

I suddenly realized this woman could help me.

"Would you like some coffee?"

"Very much so."

We walked out of the funeral parlor together. Two blocks south was a large bagel emporium. We sat down in the back with two slightly stale cups of black coffee.

"You have no idea how I shall miss that man," she said, putting on a pair of sunglasses.

"Then you kept up your friendship with Elias?" I asked.

"Not really. The last two years he was difficult. Oh, I don't really mean that. What am I saying? I'll be honest. What does it matter now! I always had a thing for that man. But he lost his head over that girl."

"You mean Terry?"

"Who else? She was too young for him. And too crazy. He did goddamn cartwheels for her. He even took a job as a doorman. Can you imagine that? Elias—in a soldier boy uniform."

"Where did he meet her?"

She laughed nastily. "I was there when he met her. She was waitressing in one of those hip new sake bars on Ninth Street. Near Second Avenue. You know the place?"

"No. I don't know much about sake."

"You're not missing anything. Anyway, there we were—Elias and I. Good friends. Actually, a little bit more than just friends. And he just flipped for her. And from what I understand, he started hanging out there, without me. And that was that."

"Does this Terry still work there?"

"No. I don't know what she does now. A few commercials once in a while, I think. She used to be part of a comedy team. I don't even know if she works at all. Probably Elias took care of her. She has a nice apartment in Manhattan Plaza; that place on West Forty-third Street reserved for actors and artists. And from what I hear, all she does is wander around and look for clothes."

"Clothes?"

"You know . . . antique clothes. Didn't you notice the kind of stuff she wears? You know . . . a Rita Hayworth sweater . . . a jacket that Mary Astor wore to a Noël Coward opening . . . that kind of stuff."

She took her glasses off.

"Why are you so interested in Terry Ray?" Laura asked, snuffling.

"It's hard to put into words."

She laughed bitterly.

"I understand exactly what you mean," she

said. And then she broke down and wept. I felt numb.

An hour later I stood in front of Detective Sofia Little's desk. It was a strangely neat and modern desk in a series of rabbit warrens called a precinct homicide squad.

She didn't seem surprised that I showed up.

"You have something to tell me about that driver's license, Miss Nestleton?"

"No."

She grinned and started to busy herself with a stapler.

"I just came from Elias Almodovar's funeral."

She didn't reply.

"I was wondering why I didn't see you there."

My question seemed to irritate her. She put the stapler down.

"And why would you expect me to attend?"

"Because I thought it was standard procedure for detectives to attend the victims' funeral as part of an ongoing investigation."

"You watch too many mafia movies. This was a mugging. We know what happened. Street muggers don't show up at the funerals of their victims."

"If, indeed, it was a street mugging," I replied.

Now she was infuriated.

"What are you talking about, Miss Nestleton! *If* it was a mugging? What the hell do you think it was? A UFO abduction? Almodovar left his job at midnight. He went to a few bars in the neighborhood. We've placed him in three . . . two on Columbus, one on Broadway. Around four-forty-five in the morning, he made his last pit stop and ended up walking on the east side of Central Park West in the sixties. Maybe he was going to cut through the park. Maybe he was heading toward the Columbus Circle subway station. Wherever he was going, he was assaulted right there . . . in a secluded area of the parking lot for Tavern on the Green, just off Central Park West. That is where he was knifed. There were three stab wounds in his body. No one saw the attack. All the evidence, however, was consistent with an armed robbery by at least one and probably two perpetrators . . . which led to resistance from the victim . . . which led to the victim's death. Do I make myself clear?"

I didn't say a word in response at first. Two facts in her monologue made me uncomfortable. One—why would a "born again" man spend the post-midnight hours in bars? Two—that parking lot he was murdered in, I knew it quite well. I had often walked through it on my way to cat-sit Frenchy. It was as if somehow I was implicated.

"Was he in those bars on the morning of the murder with his girlfriend?" I asked.

"You mean Terry Ray?"

"Yes."

"From what we have learned, he was alone. Tell me, Miss Nestleton, do you have any information on this case that you think we should know?"

"Not really."

"Well, thanks for stopping by."

I headed toward the door.

"You might be interested to know, Miss Nestleton, that the ballistic tests came back positive. The Lone Ranger is buried."

"How nice," I replied. "For everyone."

As the crow flies, it is less than a mile from Sofia Little's desk to the spot in the Tavern on the Green parking lot where Elias met his death.

As a forty-one-year-old actress walks . . . it is twenty-one blocks. And they seemed quite long and twisty ones.

The clock on the building at the southeast end of the park read thirty-four minutes past noon.

I looked around. Wisps of yellow crime scene tape were on the ground. Two spaces in the parking lot had been crudely isolated by trash cans, making a barrier. I moved past the barrier and stood where Elias had died. The street, Central Park West, was only about twenty yards away, separated from the lot by a high stone fence, and hidden by a profusion of large old trees with lush, almost violent late-spring canopies.

People were walking into the Tavern on the Green from both the street side and the park side. June at the Tavern was a big lunch month, I knew. It used to be the place where New Yorkers had sweet sixteen parties and similar celebrations. Was it still that? Most likely. But I didn't really know. I did know it had become posher and much more expensive.

I felt an indescribable sadness standing there. It came suddenly and just washed over me like a wave. I lifted my face a bit, into the breeze. Maybe he had put up only token resistance and then dropped to his knees on the hard ground to pray. And then his murderers had killed him. Maybe they had killed him simply because he had no money on him and they didn't want credit cards and such. Maybe, in fact, Elias had turned into a raging lion and forced his frightened attackers to strike and flee. Maybe the knife had been Elias's. Maybe it wasn't a robbery at all. Maybe a pigeon had flown onto his shoulder—a kind of holy ghost dancer—and the attackers had thought the pigeon was Satan and had killed Elias by mistake. Maybe . . . maybe . . . maybe . . . a thousand possible scenarios from the most plausible to the most absurd.

But what was Elias Almodovar doing wandering around the park at four-thirty in the morning? Maybe drunk. A lapse? More maybes. They flooded my head. They made me reel.

Only the trees above had seen it all . . . in the predawn darkness. I remembered those trees. Years ago, when I was taking acting lessons uptown, I used to walk in Central Park for hours. I had purchased a book called *A Guide to the Trees of Central Park.* It was a walking guide. Go to lamppost number 6705 and thirty feet south of it you will find the oldest Norway spruce in the park. Or the largest European beech. Oh, I had been a glutton for those walks. Few people know that Central Park is one of the largest tree gardens in the world. I mean large in the sense of complexity and diversity. It contains an enormous number of different native and imported trees. This was the design of its creators. And this they had accomplished.

Was that it? Had Elias come here to listen to the early-morning whispers of the branches overhead? They were like velvet brushes on snare drums.

The maybes were crushing me.

I looked at the tree canopy—intertwined, complex, sharing room. Three, four, six different kinds of trees between the street and the lot. The sad thing was, I could neither remember nor identify them.

I began to circle the death scene slowly, trying to catch something, feel something, intuit something.

It was no use.

At one-thirty that same afternoon, weary but unbowed, I stepped out of a cab at Prince Street and West Broadway, walked one block west, and purchased two large bologna sandwiches at the last working-class deli in Soho. Bologna on white with mustard, lettuce, and tomato. These monstrosities were for Sam Tully. I purchased a chicken salad on whole wheat for myself.

Then I trudged to Spring Street and rang Sam's outside bell.

He was waiting for me at the door as usual. He had a weird look on his face.

When I reached the top stairs of the landing, he asked: "Is that really you, Nestleton?"

"Do I look strange?"

"I never saw you with a hat before and I didn't figure you'd be coming up again so soon."

I snapped: "One. I just came from a funeral. Two. If my visit disturbs you, I'm sorry. I'll just go right back down."

"Damn! A huffy lady. That's all I need now. Come on in and shut up, honey."

I walked inside. Pickles was nowhere to be seen.

"The fire has gone out. I need restoking. Take a walk with me, honey, and I'll buy you a taste."

That was one thing I didn't want to do then—accompany him to one of his sleazy bars and watch him drink his poison while listening to Bobby Darin singing "Mack the Knife."

I dangled the bologna sandwiches in front of him. The poor old man teetered on a precipice of conflicting needs. He chose the bologna sandwiches, unwrapping one on his "cold" typewriter. I did not touch the chicken salad sandwich.

As he was chomping away, I told him most of what had happened since I last was in his company . . . in detail . . . with commentary. He listened politely.

When he had finished, he said, "I see this Ezekiel guy . . ."

I corrected him immediately: "Elias, not Ezekiel."

"Six of one, half dozen of another. Anyway, I see this pilgrim is sending you over the edge, honey. Leave it be. They say mugging, you say murder. Because from what you tell me, it seems like a case of criminal projection."

"What does that mean?" I asked, a bit testily.

"Simple. The bodega killing scrambled your head. You thought that bullet was meant for you. It turns out the Lone Ranger didn't know who the hell you were. So, the next killing that comes along, you just fasten all those unsheathed claws on another body. Sort of clamp down and hold on. Boy! These sandwiches are dynamite, honey."

I waited until his mouth was totally full.

"It's those bloody coincidences, Tully. My driver's license or a facsimile thereof, in his wallet. His girlfriend part of a comedy team with the daughter of the couple I was cat-sitting for . . . and the owner of an apartment in the building where Elias worked part-time. So many things. Don't you get it, Sam?"

"I get it."

"You get it, but you don't sanction it."

"Sanction? I'm not the U.N."

He finished one sandwich completely. He asked: "Do you think Pickles would like bologna?"

"Don't even think of giving it to him, Sam."

"Okay."

"There's something I didn't tell you."

"What?"

"I went to the crime scene."

"Okay."

"And I just stood there."

"Okay."

"You know why I went there?"

"Because it is a crime scene."

"No. Yes. No. Stop making jokes, Sam. I went there not because I expected to find something the NYPD missed. It was because of what you once told me about your goofy sleuth Harry Bondo."

"No one calls Harry Bondo goofy and lives to tell about it."

I ignored the threat.

"You said that Harry had developed a way to stand silently at a crime scene, even months after the crime occurred, and extract something important. An almost mystical communion."

"The man can sure do that, but remember, honey, Bondo ain't a psychic."

"It didn't work with me, Sam."

"Maybe you were facing the wrong way. If I remember right, that happened in the second book in the series and Harry was facing southeast. Were you facing in that direction?"

It was futile to continue that particular conversation with him.

"There's something else I haven't told you, Sam."

"Go ahead, change the subject. It's an old chick trick."

"You call me a chick again, Sam, and I'll repossess your second bologna sandwich."

"Be compassionate, Nestleton. Remember my age."

"I'm in love, Sam."

"Whoa!" he blurted out and then stared at me fiercely. There was a long, awkward silence.

Then I added: "But I'm not absolutely sure."

"Is that right?"

"Yes."

"I take it, honey, that the object of this love or whatever it is . . . is not that Marcello Mastroianni character you usually hang out with but who is now floating somewhere north of here looking after pretty young actresses in training."

"You are correct."

"Then I see you got a problem."

"I slept with him once."

"I ain't your priest."

"It all happened so suddenly."

"Who is he?"

"Beatrice Woburn's lawyer."

"Well, at least he can afford you."

"Actually, he's financially strapped. And his passion isn't law . . . it's criminology."

"You're kidding me, honey."

"No. The truth."

"No one uses that word anymore . . . criminology."

"He does, Sam. He's kind of old-fashioned. Right now he's engaged in a long research project on just who assassinated Abe Lincoln and why."

"I thought that case was closed."

"So did I."

"No offense. But he seems to be playing with fifty-one cards. And that's being generous."

"He's gentle. He's strangely exciting. He makes me feel very young, Sam. Almost frivolous."

"A frivolous cat woman? That'll be the day."

"I want to eat cotton candy and candied apples on sticks."

"Lord help us."

Pickles jumped through the open window, strode aggressively across the room, leaped onto Sam's table, and began to worry the remaining bologna sandwich.

"You think Pickles will ever be born again?" Sam asked.

It was time to leave. I walked home slowly, removing my hat on the way. The confession had made me feel much better.

I embraced my cats mightily when I got into

the loft. There was a brief phone message from Nora. She was still on Martha's Vineyard.

There was nothing from Tony. I realized that I should write him or call him, but I didn't.

Instead, I called A.G. Roth. He was out. I told the machine that I was sorry I left so abruptly the night before, that it was not his fault, and that, in a sense, I longed to see him again.

After I hung up, I was embarrassed. To use the phrase "long for" was childish and excessive. But Alice, I chided myself . . . isn't that love?

Then I undressed, showered, ate the chicken salad sandwich and plotted my next move in the case of Terry Ray.

Chapter 8

"I need a favor," I said to my agent, Madge Lyphard. It was nine-thirty the next morning in her office on West Fifty-seventh Street. My plan had been formulated . . . my investigation mapped out . . . my prospects, to say the least, were dim.

Madge was not yet awake. I was wide awake.

"I usually don't get in this early," she noted.

"Oh, I'm aware of that," I replied. Her eyes narrowed. Madge Lyphard had been my agent for the past two years.

As actors' agents go, she was fine, and par for the course. She had gotten me just two television commercial jobs in that time and one small role playing a drunken socialite in an independent film. She was always, so she said, hot on the trail of a well-paying minor role for me in a soap opera.

Whatever else I had done in the theater in the

past two years had come about because of my efforts or through blind luck.

But don't get me wrong. I liked her very much.

"A favor is a favor is a favor," she intoned, dripping brown sugar into her coffee.

Then she sat and waited. Madge was small, pretty, pugnacious, a few years younger than myself. Her desk was a blitz of papers. Her walls were covered for reasons unknown with grim crime scene photos of the New York of the late forties and early fifties. They were disturbing yet somehow fitting for an agent.

I spun out my lie.

"As you know, Madge, I do some cat sitting on the side. Right now I'm working for a lovely woman, lovely but sad. She has a daughter who hates her. A comedienne. The woman told me she longs for a photo of her daughter working. I want to get her one, as a gift, for being so kind to me."

Then I gave her a piece of paper with the name "Rachel Woburn" written on it, before I continued.

"She used to be part of a comedy team. Maybe that's all you can get. Even a publicity photo of the team would be fine."

"What name did the team perform under?" Madge asked.

"Don't know. Maybe Woburn and Ray."

"Okay. Not a problem. I'll make some calls. When do you want it?"

"Now."

She glared at me. The favor was beginning to rankle her.

"Okay. Get back to me around noon."

I went into Central Park to waste some time. I sat in the zoo café and sipped a coffee. Yes. I was now embarked on a carefully thought out plan, the purpose of which was to tie that Ray woman to a murder conspiracy.

Sitting there, on that bright morning in the open air, I felt the stirrings of doubt.

Sam had said I had nothing and was acting up because of the bodega incident . . . a kind of unresolved lingering shock.

So he said. I knew, however, that coincidences were not "nothing."

But something else was bothering me. My plan basically consisted of probing the head and heart of Terry Ray.

And the mode of attack was through her passion, as Laura Arroyo had outlined it—antique clothing.

This was standard operating procedure for an investigator on the wrong side of respectability. I had to mine the crumbs that neither the homicide detectives nor a PI would stoop to gather up.

Of course, I know some things other people don't know, because I'm an actress and therefore have an inordinate respect for artifice . . . and antique clothing is an artifice of a special, crucial kind to many women.

What really bothered me was: Was I off on an elaborate wild-goose chase that had been set into motion by my discomfort over the A.G. Roth thing?

Was it a kind of "flight" response?

After all, what was Elias to me? And what had I been to him? Nothing but a pleasant memory after years of not seeing each other.

After all, why had this Terry Ray affected me so strongly? She surely had. I didn't like her. I didn't trust her. And I had only met her twice. Was it the bizarre eye makeup? Did I think she was a tramp? Was she the tramp lurking in me? Did I think, subconsciously, that I was a tramp for my adventure with A.G. Roth . . . an adventure that I knew was still unfolding?

Tony had once told me that he knew the way I was going to die. I was going to become obsessed by an intuition, follow that intuition, which would be without any substance whatsoever, and end up facing a total stranger in an abandoned theater, whereupon said stranger would calmly blow me to kingdom come.

But then again, Tony made many outlandish predictions. And none of them had ever come true—not yet.

I decided to go into the zoo. I paid my admission and sat down in the chilly dark penguin house . . . staring at the colony of penguins behind protective glass.

They cavorted in and out of the water and they calmed me. I wondered what would happen if Sam's cat Pickles by chance met up with a full-grown penguin—just saw one waddling toward him. Pickles, no doubt, would consider the flightless bird fair game. This, of course, would be a mistake. Pickles would get trounced. But what kind of beast would the penguin think Pickles was? A leopard seal? A grounded killer whale? Perhaps.

I dawdled in the zoo for two hours, then called Madge. She had performed magnificently; a publicity photo of the team could be picked up from Rachel's agent on West Forty-third Street. At the desk.

I thanked Dear Madge profusely, followed instructions, and picked up the photo at the desk. It was encased, absurdly, in one of those huge thin brown envelopes . . . the kind medical X-rays come in.

Package in hand, I brazenly entered a glittering new bar on Forty-third Street and Tenth Avenue, sat down at the bar, and ordered a ginger ale with a piece of lime.

It was not quite noon.

I slid the photo out of the envelope and studied it. A typical publicity photo. The twisted sisters faced each other, glossily, almost three-quarters face. Terry on the left; Rachel on the right. Just a little more than a head shot. Rachel wore a turtle neck. Terry wore a blouse with a high neck and frills.

The name of the group had been Baby Sister. It was an odd name for a comedy team. Maybe that was what their most famous skit was about—a baby sister. It didn't matter, really. The team was, obviously, now moribund.

I slipped the photo back into the envelope and took out my secret list. I spread it on the top of the bar and studied it.

All it contained was the names and addresses of three antique clothing stores. They were the ones I had selected from memory and the yellow pages as the ones that Terry Ray would most probably frequent.

One in Soho—called Brass.

One in the East Village called the Pink Hippo.

One on Second Avenue in the Thirties called Star Quality.

If I was wrong, I would expand the list. Given where I was, I chose the Soho place first. This would only require a trip downtown on the Ninth Avenue bus and then a brisk walk.

It was, in fact, a quite pleasant ride downtown. I got off at Abington Square and then walked south and east into Soho.

Brass was a loft on Wooster Street—a large loft. There was no tumult about the place. In fact, it was set up like a regular retail establishment.

The clothes hung on hangers on large brass racks. And the clothes were impressive: flapper evening gowns . . . brocaded dresses . . . sportswear from the 1940s, tartan skirts that Mount Holyoke coeds used to wear with their cashmere sweaters. And a whole lot more. For some reason their mode of presentation made me uncomfortable.

There were accessories also, in deep shelves along one wall. A single object in a single pigeonhole. Like Egyptian artifacts in a museum. Among them were hats, gloves, pocketbooks, and even white silk opera scarves.

There were two other customers in the loft. The proprietor—I assumed she was the proprietor—was behind a counter near the door. She was doing the *Times* crossword puzzle.

I slipped into my role. It is amazing how fast I

can do that—still. The understudy's hard-earned trick. Button, button, who's got the button.

First I started to make a little noise, just a little . . . moving the hangars on the racks . . . a sweet, sliding, bristling sound.

One of the customers left. Not, I hope, because of my act.

Then I upped the ante a bit. Body language, of course. Face a bit contorted, a bit strained. A whole series of jerky arm and leg movements.

What I was striving for, of course, was that hoary stereotype—the confused shopper who wants to buy.

In other words—I was seriously looking for something I simply couldn't find.

Like the critics say: Alice Nestleton is a fine actress, when she works. She was working then. And it worked!

"Can I help you?" the crossword puzzle woman inquired. She was now standing a few feet to my left, anxious to help, very much the good saleswoman.

"Yes. Yes. I hope so. I am trying to find a gift for a friend. She shops here all the time. She loves your stuff. I just can't figure out what to get her. I mean . . ." And then I threw up my hands.

The saleswoman mulled the problem. I pressed on.

"You must know her. Terry Ray. Maybe if you tell me what she likes . . . ."

"The name doesn't ring a bell," said the saleswoman.

I slipped the photo out of the envelope.

"The one on the left," I said.

"Oh, of course I know her." Her face lit up. "She's here often. A lovely young woman."

"It would help me if you can remember."

"But I just told you, miss. I do remember her."

"I mean what she purchased.."

"While she was often here, she didn't make that many purchases. A small beaded purse if I remember. And one of those cashmere sweaters. What she really wanted wasn't the kind of merchandise we handle. She was really interested in bell bottom jeans à la 1960 or 1970."

I thanked her from the bottom of my thespian heart for her help and assured her that it would somehow facilitate my purchases.

The moment she went back to her crossword, I slipped out.

The Pink Hippo in the East Village was an entirely different kettle of fish. It was low-ceilinged, funky, filled with everything from cut-down, cut-out jeans to Janis Joplin boas to elevator shoes to hats with lights.

It was all 1960s and 1970s, presented in the glare of twisting strobe lights and loud music.

It was dazzling. I just stood there, in awe. Antique clothing stores always, in a sense, awed me. I could never figure out where they got all those clothes.

No doubt some came from thrift stores—but not in Manhattan, where the antique stuff is immediately winnowed out by a horde of knowledgeable hunters.

No doubt some came from mysterious wholesalers.

No doubt some came from friends.

No doubt some came from auctions and garage sales. Everyone has some clothes in a closet from a dead relative that they want to get rid of.

And, no doubt, some came from nefarious manufacturers who produce new garments and sell them as old garments.

Tony loved to retail the story of a larcenous uncle of his who tried to make a living selling bogus antique clothes. After World War II there was a tremendous growth in army surplus stores. The most popular items were from the Pacific War and had to do with U.S. Marine apparel.

Specially sought after were marine web belts on which marines in combat affixed their bayonets, canteens, and side arms.

Alas, the stocks of surplus web belts soon ran out and a whole host of manufacturers rushed in. Tony's uncle was one of these. The problem was, he manufactured the belts so fast he forgot to put fasteners on them.

I looked around. It would be very easy to fake 1960s- and 1970s-type clothing. But all of the stuff in the Pink Hippo looked authentic.

There were two salespeople: a young woman in jeans and high heels and a middle-aged man with puffy 1970s sideburns.

I went into my act. It should have worked well because the space was smaller than Brass and I was the only customer in the store.

Alas, perhaps because of the music, perhaps because of the fact that the two salespersons were now sipping what looked like iced coffee behind a counter and gesticulating over some catalogs—my act didn't go over.

I was ignored. Two more customers came in. Young girls. They were fascinated by the platform sneakers and the hooker high heels with whit teardrops on red satin stretched over the incredible narrow bridges of the shoes.

My act would never work in this theater, I realized.

So I walked over to the counter. Business cards were in a small rack. I took one. The proprietor of the Pink Hippo, according to the card, was one Arlene Boccio.

I decided it must be the female of the iced coffee pair behind the counter. I was correct. She walked over to me, smiling, after I called her name.

"Look," I said, "I have a friend of mine who shops here often. She likes bell bottom jeans. Anyway, I have to get her a birthday gift and I simply don't know what the hell to get her. Can you tell me what else she buys so I don't duplicate anything?"

"Sure. If I remember the customer."

"Oh, I'm sure you will. Her name is Terry. Tall girl, heavy makeup around the eyes. A kind of Southern accent. She's a comedienne."

Arlene Boccio didn't think long. "I don't remember her."

"Surely there can't be too many customers always anxious for bell bottom jeans," I protested, with a whine.

"You'd be surprised," she said huffily. "Sorry." She headed back toward her sideburned companion.

"Wait! I have a picture of her."

I took the photo out and thrust it toward her. "The one on the left," I said.

She looked. She shook her head. She said "sorry" again and continued her journey.

"Wait! Are you sure?"

"Didn't you hear me? I told you I don't know any customer named Terry Ray. I don't know your friend."

I put the photo back and glumly headed for the door.

My step, however, became slower and slower. Something was very wrong. I distinctly remembered saying the name "Terry." Only Terry. This woman had used the full name—"Terry Ray."

But maybe she had read the credits on the photo. It was possible. Barely possible. The writing was small.

I had to think. If she was lying . . . why?

There was a large poster on the wall. I stopped in front of it to give myself time to figure out how to proceed with the situation.

The poster, I realized, was an advertisement for a show in an art gallery.

First, the last names of the artists . . . as if they were famous. Maybe they were, but I didn't know them.

Lorimer
Appel
Torg
Devlin
Smith
Arthur
Wolff

Then there was a photographic reproduction of one of the exhibits in the show. It was quite beautiful: freestanding sculpture of a sort. Five stick figures, each one at least seven feet tall. The stick frame was bamboo. On each frame hung a beautiful silk kimono.

It looked like five cosmic scarecrows doing a macabre dance.

Then came the announcement of the show. It made me wince.

> BEATRICE WOBURN PRESENTS . . .
> Mind and Material
> THE WORLD OF THE VANGUARD FABRIC ARTIST

I stepped back. This was, I realized, the burned-out show that A.G. Roth had spoken about when he was recounting poor Beatrice's woes.

Another coincidence. I was being drowned by them.

Suddenly I remembered Sam Tully's warning . . . that I was obsessed with Elias's death because of the bodega incident.

I had scoffed at the warning then. But now I became just a bit uneasy. Was my mind making connections that weren't there?

A very funny scenario popped into my head.

Maybe I was chasing Terry Ray because her eye makeup reminded me of the masked bodega shooter—the Lone Ranger.

Wouldn't that be a hoot?

I gathered my faculties, studied the poster again, made note of the name and address of the gallery, and walked out of the Pink Hippo.

On the street I wavered. Which was more important? The art gallery or the unvisited vintage clothing store on my list?

If Arlene Boccio had lied to me—the gallery.

And she had, I decided.

Chapter 9

The gallery was called Patroclus. It was on Bond Street, near the Bowery.

Of course, there was really no gallery left—just four parched walls, a burned ceiling, and the astonishing wreckage that always seemed to accumulate after a fire is put out.

The inside of the space was noisy with workmen and their tools. There was no door or windows anymore; one just walked over a ledge from the sidewalk and one was inside the gallery space.

A carpenter with as beautiful a torso as I've ever seen on a living man was sipping coffee very close to where I stepped inside. He wore one of those strange chastity belts with hammers hanging on the sides and deep pockets for nails. I wondered for a salacious moment if the man ever heard of the old rural saying: "He's as dumb as a bag of hammers." Of course, it was entirely possible that he was one of those many out-of-work PhDs in philosophy.

"Do you know the name of the gallery owner?" I asked the man sweetly.

"Are you from the City?"

"You mean officially?"

"Yeah."

"No. Just a friend of a friend."

"Than her name is Robin Herrara and there she is."

He pointed to the woman at the back of the space who was inspecting panels of sideboards. She was a stocky woman with unruly black hair protruding from a painter's cap.

I approached her and immediately went into my wide-eyed routine.

"What happened here? My God! What happened?"

"A fire," she said evenly, as if she was weary of telling the story over and over again.

"I came in from New Jersey to see the show. And well . . . it's . . . when . . . did it just happen? I heard nothing about it."

"A few weeks ago," she replied.

She started to stand the boards upright against the wall. It was obvious she didn't want to carry on any further conversation with this New Jersey matron—me.

Breathlessly, still reeling from the bogus shock, I asked: "Was anyone hurt?"

Robin Herrara gave me a hard glare, as if she finally realized that this stranger would have to be dealt with as gently but as firmly as possible so she could get on with the reconstruction of the gallery.

"No one, from what we know. It started in the next building, second floor. An attempted robbery at a garment manufacturing firm. From Hong Kong. They made wedding dresses. The thieves were going for a safe, we hear. They used a torch. It blew up. There was a fire. It spread to this building. Two firemen were overcome by smoke but that's all. Nobody lives in these buildings and the robbery was at night. Everything was burned to a crisp. The show. The furnishings. Everything. It was a short, ugly conflagration." She smiled and paused. "So here we are." And then she put her hands on her hips a bit pugnaciously, as if to say, "Okay, nosey lady . . . there it is . . . all of it . . . are you satisfied? Now, will you please go back to Jersey?"

I was not ready to quit, no matter my persona.

"I'm so disappointed. My friend was exhibiting in the show."

"You mean Mind and Material?"

"Yes. Yes. Terry Ray."

The woman looked perplexed.

"There was no artist named Terry Ray exhibiting in that show."

"Are you sure?"

"Of course I'm sure. This is my gallery."

"But . . ." I feigned total confusion. "Maybe . . . well . . . maybe Terry used a pseudonym."

Then I slipped the photo out of the envelope. "The one on the left is Terry Ray."

"That woman was not exhibiting in the show," she said. She tapped the photo. "Nor was the other one. But her at least I know. That's Rachel, Bea Woburn's daughter. Do you know her?"

"Not really," I replied. And then I did a slow pirouette as if marveling at the horror of it all . . . the fire . . . the destruction. "You say all the artwork went up in smoke?"

"Yes. All."

"I wonder," I said, "if I have the wrong show and the wrong gallery."

Robin Herrara found that very amusing indeed.

I was just buying time. Since I really didn't know why I was there and what I was looking for . . . I certainly didn't know how to proceed further.

The only thing I had learned was that the owner of the gallery where Bea Woburn's curated show would have taken place did not know Terry Ray and did know Rachel Woburn. So what?

Suddenly I asked: "Is Arlene Boccio a friend of yours?"

"I don't know the name."

"Elias Almodovar?"

"Who?"

That was when I stepped out of the burned-out perimeter and onto the street.

Meandering for a few moments under a cloudy sky, I found myself walking up Third Avenue.

The thought came to me that while my head didn't know where I was going . . . my feet surely did.

Oh Alice! What has gotten into you! You are forty-one years old!

Is he home? Will he be home? How can he not be home?

Was he waiting for my call?

Was he sitting by the damn phone?

I stood by the pay phone across the street from A.G. Roth's apartment building.

The quarter was in one hand.

My other hand was on the receiver.

It was strange how quickly my investigation had dissolved . . . a few antique clothing stores . . . a gallery . . . and then . . . poof . . . up in proverbial smoke.

When the smoke had settled, there I was. A supplicant.

I dropped the quarter and a dime into the slot and dialed.

He picked up the phone on the first ring. He was waiting. He knew. I knew. This was, as they say, an inexorable relationship. Like two ships in the arctic night that, despite their high-tech radar, cannot help but collide. Oh, the ludicrous images were coming thick and fast.

"Alice?" His voice was a bit desperate. It sounded the way I wanted it to sound.

"Yes."

"Where are you?"

"Downstairs."

"Are you coming up?"

"Yes."

"When?" He almost spat the question out over the phone. I had just a brief desire to tease him—but it fled.

"Now."

When I walked out of the elevator on his floor, he was waiting for me by the door.

I hesitated. What madness was this? Yes, I had slept with him once. It was understandable. I was very, very lonely.

But this was something else. This was trouble,

I knew. My feelings were volcanic but inchoate. I was a fool, bubbling over one minute, analytical the next.

All we did was shake hands primly. I intuited his nervousness.

The drawings he had purchased from London were scattered over the living room rug. As if he was an interior decorator selecting fabrics. Didn't the man ever do anything relating to his legal profession?

He took my arm and guided me over to one of them.

"Look!" he ordered.

"I'm looking. But I saw it the last time I was here."

"Look closely. The drawing is absurd. Even the English must have known at the time that Lincoln never saw his assassin; that he was shot in the back of the head. But here we have Lincoln and Booth gazing at each other before the shot is fired. A kind of dramatic confrontation. All kinds of torment and history in the gazes. Don't you agree?"

"Yes. There is torment."

"But I'll tell you something," he said, gripping my arm hard. "Sometimes you can learn more from a fantastical representation than from a photo."

"That is a very unlawyerly observation," I noted.

He kissed me. I kissed him back. He smelled of shaving lotion. I didn't mind at all. The fingers of my right hand traced the contours of his cheekbone. I felt lightheaded.

We disengaged.

"Do you know why the Lincoln assassination intrigues me?"

"No."

"Because unlike other assassinations, it truly changed the course of history. Kennedy's assassination was horrendous. And his brother's. And Martin Luther King's. But Lincoln was a whole different story. We would be a different nation if Lincoln had not been assassinated."

"How different?"

"I don't know."

"But you do believe that Booth and his associates conspired to murder Lincoln and carried it out? You do believe that, don't you, A.G.?"

"No."

"Who then?"

"This is not clear to me yet. I've only been working on it for some nine years."

I laughed, moved closer, and tousled his hair.

"Is it possible, my dear Counselor Roth, that you have become, despite your denials, a conspiracy kook?"

He grinned. "And I thought you were attracted to me because of my mind . . . my abilities to see through the fog of history . . . my razorlike acumen."

"Actually, it's your money."

Then, I am a bit embarrassed to admit, we made love right there and then, on the floor, on the rug, scattering and bruising all those precious assassination drawings from the London newspapers of so long ago.

Forgive me, Honest Abe. I have sinned.

After the debauch I went into the bedroom and fell fast asleep in A.G.'s bed.

I slept until 6 P.M. When I awoke, A.G. was by the door.

"Do you often stare at sleeping women?" I asked.

"No, but we're lovers now. Real, old-fashioned, star-crossed lovers. That gives me the right."

"We made love twice, A.G. Only twice—and once on the floor."

"Exactly. It was the floor that contained the truth. When sober, middle-aged people are so swept up they do it on the floor . . . there is no doubt about the situation."

"Sometimes, A.G., I don't know when you are serious."

"Neither do I. Can I make you some coffee?"

"No. I have to go home."

He nodded in his understanding fashion, and vanished from the door. It occurred to me that this might be the first man I had ever been intimate with who was basically less experienced than I in affairs of the heart.

When I had located all my clothes, dressed, and fixed myself up, I walked into the living room.

A.G. was once again studying that British assassination drawing.

"Can I peel you an orange?" he asked.

"No."

"Can I write you a poem?"

"No."

"Can I thank you from the bottom of my heart for coming here today?"

"No."

"Can I beg you on hands and knees to see me tomorrow?"

"No."

"Can I tell you something about this drawing?"

"We already discussed it."

"Ah, Alice. It was a very preliminary, unsatisfactory discussion. I want to spruce up my criminological reputation."

I smiled. It was my criminological reputation

that needed enhancement. My investigation had ended ignominiously, in a burned-out art gallery.

"Look at it again, Alice."

I did.

"We agree that the drawing is nonsensical—don't we, Alice? Everyone knows that the shooter was behind the president; that Lincoln never saw his assassin."

"Yes, we agree on that."

"What if this drawing, unlike the others, had been done before the assassination?"

"That doesn't make sense. All the drawings were made in London after the reports of the assassination reached them. You told me that yourself, A.G."

"It doesn't make sense if you buy the story in history books."

"And I know you don't, A.G."

"Not only don't I—but I have an intelligent alternative. Which is why I'm not what you'd call a conspiracy kook."

"I'm listening."

"Do you know England's stance toward the two protagonists in the American Civil War?"

"Not really."

"Very pro-Confederacy. England needed the Southern cotton for their mills. And the North was blockading the Confederacy. Only toward the end of the war, when the British realized the South would lose, did they become neutral."

"So?"

"During the period of British support of the Confederacy, the British secret service was operating in the United States, particularly in the North, coordinating 'copperhead' sentiment, meaning anti-Union conspirators."

"So?"

"So I believe the British secret service planned the assassination of Lincoln. And this drawing is not an attempt to report the event after it happened. It was drawn months before the assassination, as part of the assassination plans." He smiled. "What do you think?"

"I have two questions."

"Go ahead."

"One: How do you know the drawing was done before the assassination?"

"I don't."

"And two: Why in heaven's name would the British want to assassinate Lincoln after the war was over? What were the benefits?"

"I haven't the slightest idea."

I walked over and kissed him on the cheek, almost sisterly.

"Well then, A.G., until you answer those two questions, I am afraid you are a conspiracy kook."

He held me tightly.

"I have to go," I said.

"We are lovers, aren't we?"

I disengaged and hurried out.

When I opened the door of my loft and saw Bushy and Pancho seated together, calmly, on a window ledge, I felt a sense of dread.

That feeling, dread, stemmed from my belief in cat "astrology." Oh, this has nothing to do with the planetary kind. It simply means that when there is a conjunction of usually disjunctive felines—a person is in trouble.

Bushy and Pancho do not hang out together. In fact, they usually go to great lengths to avoid each other. But there they were, seated calmly and close.

I looked quickly around, and my eyes caught the blink of the telephone answering machine. Menacing. It was menacing.

I closed the door softly behind me and began to circle the machine. The felines kept their eyes on me. They made no sign. They knew the light was menacing. They were warning me with their absolute silence.

I played the message.

"Hello, Miss Nestleton. This is Paulus Darien. It is five-thirty P.M. It is imperative that you go to the Woburn apartment the moment you receive this message. I repeat, it is imperative."

That was all. How strange it was. I had just come from the apartment of Bea Woburn's lawyer. And a phone call was waiting for me from Sidney Woburn's lawyer. It seemed I could not escape from the Woburns. What did they want now? A cleaning lady?

This star-crossed lover turned grumpy. Should I ignore the message? Call the apartment? Do nothing?

My body was beginning to ache a bit. Making love on a floor was not therapeutic for a budding actress like myself.

I rewound the tape and played the message again. That lawyer seemed to be quite serious. Almost threatening.

I thought about it for a half hour while eating a piece of cold chicken, then took a cab uptown.

The regular doorman, who knew me quite well, didn't say a word. He just ushered me in.

Even when I asked him directly: "Do you know what is going on? Is something going on?" he just shook his head grimly. I wondered why I had not seen him at Elias's funeral.

Once I entered the apartment, I was treated to an astonishing sight.

Sidney Woburn was on one side of the room, standing rigid.

On the other side of the room, equally rigid, was Beatrice Woburn—thin, hawklike, short gray hair, wearing what could only be described as a potter's smock.

In the center of the room, seated, was the lawyer Darien. He seemed to be playing the role of Marshal Earp in Tombstone, keeping the gunfighters apart.

The room was crackling with hostility.

"Thank you for coming," the lawyer said.

"What is going on?" I asked.

Beatrice mocked me in a screaming voice: "What is going on? Look!"

She was pointing to one of the small elegant matching chairs at the entrance to the living room.

There was a cat on the chair, in a grooming mode, seemingly oblivious to the onlookers.

It was not Frenchy.

It was a large bedraggled gray tabby Tom who looked, to be quite honest, like he had been plucked quite recently from a very seedy alley.

"Who is that?" I asked, confused.

"You tell me," said the lawyer.

"Where is Frenchy?" I asked.

"Frenchy is gone."

"Gone where?"

"You tell me."

I sat down on the sofa next to the lawyer.

"Do you have anything to do with this?" Darien asked me.

"I don't know what you're talking about," I replied, keeping my eyes on the cat in the chair.

"I will be brief and to the point, Miss Nestleton. Sometime this afternoon a strange young woman entered the building and claimed to be Frenchy's new cat-sitter. She carried another cat in a carrier. She told the doorman, who had never seen her before, that she was bringing in a friend to play with Frenchy. Since she had a key to the apartment, the doorman was not suspicious. Once she was inside the apartment, it is obvious what happened. She let her cat out—the cat you see on the chair—and put Frenchy in the carrier. Then she left the building."

The moment Darien had finished his bizarre narrative, Sidney Woburn pointed his finger at me. "It was her. I know it was her." His voice was low but bitter.

"Please," I replied, "the doormen know me. They would have recognized me. And why would I want to take Frenchy?"

Sidney's voice escalated. "You paid someone to do it! That was it. You *paid* someone!"

This was getting stupid.

"Where is A.G. Roth?" Bea asked.

"I left a message on his machine," Darien said.

"Where is Rachel? Where is Anton? Where are my children?" Bea asked, her voice rising in a kind of hysteria.

"Oh shut up!" Sidney shouted at her from across the room.

"Calm down. Please!" Darien was trying to prevent an altercation. Then he fixed his eyes on me. "I don't want to call the police."

"Are you threatening me? Call all the police you want. I told you: I had nothing to do with this."

My protestations did not seem to satisfy anyone.

"Look," I continued in a quieter, calmer tone, "it could have been Terry Ray or Rachel Woburn. They both have access to keys."

"Who is Terry Ray?" Darien asked.

"A girlfriend of a substitute doorman in this building. And an old colleague of Rachel."

"The doorman would know them both."

He was right. Besides, I realized, it seemed rather outlandish that either of them would steal Frenchy and leave a bedraggled hostage in her place.

The cat climbed down off the chair and began to amble. He had that alley cat swagger, as if he had decided he might as well make the best of his new situation.

"I don't think anyone should take this seriously," I said. "It's probably some kind of prank. That's all."

Beatrice wasn't listening to me. She seemed to shrink away from the cat. Then she pointed at Sidney Woburn across the room and called out, "I curse you for all this. For everything. You are an evil, stupid man. Everything you touch is poisoned. Cats. Children. Work. Joy. Everything."

Sidney's answer to the charges was to pick up a small blue antique clock and fling it across the room at his wife's head.

It missed.

Darien quickly stood up, took Sidney by the arm, and escorted him into the bedroom to cool off.

I was alone with Beatrice Woburn and the prowling alley cat. I peered into the kitchen for a moment. Frenchy's food and water dishes were intact, full.

Mr. Smith, as I decided to instantly name the feline stranger, would not be wanting.

Bea was getting more and more distraught. She approached me suddenly. To be honest, I was a bit frightened. Her face was contorted . . . as if someone were pinching her.

But when she was right beside me, her face softened. All I saw was sorrow.

At that moment, Mr. Smith walked past us, almost leisurely, and headed into the kitchen to inspect the bowls.

He had a very long thick tail, much darker than his body, and he carried it high. His ears seemed to twitch independently in rhythm with the tail.

"Who are you?" Bea whispered to me.

"Who *am* I?" What do you mean? You know who I am. I used to be your cat sitter."

She put her hand on my arm, with an odd kind of compassion, like I was a demented fool.

"Tell me the truth," she insisted.

"I am telling you the truth. I am Alice Nestleton. What's the matter with you? We've met before. I used to cat-sit for Frenchy."

"Did you love her?"

"Frenchy? Of course."

"Why have they done this to me?"

"Nothing has been done to you here, Mrs. Woburn. As I said, it seems to be a prank. Frenchy will be returned."

"You don't know that. You're just talking."

I didn't answer. I looked into the kitchen. Mr. Smith was sampling the dishes. I looked up. Beatrice Woburn's eyes were closed now. She swayed a little.

"Why don't you sit down," I suggested. The voices from the bedroom were getting louder and angrier.

Beatrice started to speak in a low voice. "When a woman loathes her husband but can't leave him, because of children or fear or cowardice—what can she do? She can seek out lovers, alcohol, friends, hobbies, passions, God, shrinks. I tried everything. They never brought me peace. Only Frenchy did. I confided in her, Miss Nestleton. Since she was a kitten. Just looking at her gave me strength. Sometimes, at night, I would be lying in bed with Sidney beside me. And I would contemplate suicide. I would think how easy and wonderful it would be to just run across the apartment, shield my face with my hands, and crash through the window to the street below.

"Do you know how many times I thought of that? What saved me was Frenchy. Sometimes, at night, I would hear her in the living room chasing her toy mice. She always played at night. And just the sound of the kitty playing; those strange, muffled thumps, would give me a kind of quiet, an acceptance, a hope. Do you see?

"Frenchy . . . she's a dear sweet little blue lady, but she's a rock. She never was just a cat to me. She was beauty and truth. She is survival.

She is, as funny as it may seem to you, my muse."

I felt too sad to reply. She started to speak again but stopped when Sidney and Darien came back into the living room.

The lawyer said, "We have decided on a course of action, Bea. If it is agreeable to you."

"I'm listening," she said quietly, keeping her eyes averted from her husband—as his were from hers.

The hatred between them was so strong, it seemed to be a literal, choking presence in the room.

Darien outlined the plan.

"Since Miss Nestleton resigned, we have used only three people to take care of Frenchy while we were searching for a replacement. Who were they? The daytime doorman. A young college student staying with a family on this floor. And the live-in maid from the penthouse. I will question all of them. If no answers are forthcoming, I will contact the police."

He waited for an answer.

"Fine," said Bea.

The lawyer waited for Sidney's public affirmation.

But Sidney did not say a word. He looked crushed. His eyes kept darting from side to side, as if searching for a glimpse of a hidden Frenchy.

The odd thing is, I followed his eyes. Everyone craved to catch a glimpse of little Frenchy. Everyone hoped she would just emerge from somewhere—unscathed and unfazed.

The cat ambled back into the living room, walked to his chair, then hopped up and began to groom himself.

I wanted to walk over to him, pick him up, look him in the eye, and ask "Who are you, Mr. Smith? Who brought you here? Where is Frenchy? Who's the prankster, Mr. Smith? And what's the point of so cruel a prank?"

Mr. Smith knew I was thinking of him. As he groomed, he shot me a defiant glance, daring me.

"Well, thank you for coming, Miss Nestleton," Darien said.

There was nothing more for me to say. I walked out, took a cab home, and fell into bed.

My kitties were a bit standoffish. They knew now that bad things were happening.

Please don't get me wrong, they were in solidarity with me, and with Frenchy, but they were a little scared of Mr. Smith. Remember, they always know everything that was happening to me.

That night I took two Tylenol PMs in order to get to sleep.

I dreamed about the Lincoln assassination. Only the occupants of that box in that theater on that night were A.G. Roth and myself.

And the shooter was, I think, Elias Almodovar.

Chapter 10

There was no time to lose. Too much had happened. No more dilettantism. No more happy meanderings among the clothes racks playing roles.

It was time to get down to steel tacks.

There were many reasons for this call to action—but the most relevant reason was my realization, when I woke up the next morning, that my comments to the lawyer characterizing the cat substitution as a prank were ridiculous.

Frenchy's disappearance was no prank.

It was a very serious threat.

And that threat had something to do with the death of Elias Almodovar.

And the death of Elias Almodovar had something to do with a can of worms I had not yet opened because I hadn't yet found the can opener that fit.

I went to Sam Tully's apartment at ten-thirty

that morning. I brought him the kind of ugly cheese Danish he craves. And I asked for his help, his immediate and concentrated help, on the case—after I had presented the latest malevolent wrinkles.

He agreed that the Frenchy "lift" was a threat.

He agreed to help me, mainly because he had reached a blank wall after some seventy pages of his new potboiler. The keys were cold.

And he agreed with my thesis that the catnapping and substitution of Mr. Smith had created a time element.

We had a ticking clock. Maybe a time bomb.

Unless of course the whole thing was nonsense . . . a Mickey Mouse clock. In which case Elias had been murdered by muggers . . . there was a nontoxic explanation for the bogus driver's license . . . Terry Ray was not evil and the association with Rachel Woburn totally innocent . . . the Frenchy lift was a prank . . . the antique clothes dealer had not lied to me . . . and "born again" actors have no special behavioral traits such as honesty or pacifism.

It was Sam who evoked the above Mickey Mouse scenario. Yes, he had such a sweet way of putting things.

Anyway, after he had finished that dreadful Danish; after he had drunk several cups of coffee with half and half and sugar; and after he had fed Pickles an astonishingly complex meal of indescribable cow and fish parts—we went for a walk.

It was Tully's belief that all the logical reasoning that forms the latticework of a criminal investigation should take place while walking, or drinking alcoholic beverages.

This, he claimed, was a philosophical tradition he had kept intact from the ancient Greeks.

In fact, his fictional gumshoe, Harry Bondo, once said: "Listen, stupid! Only the hippest perambulate."

So we headed west on Spring Street, arm in arm.

"What kind of procedure do you have in mind, honey?"

"Procedure?"

"I mean—do we do this elegantly? Or do we rip into it with fangs bared, tooth and claw?"

"Perhaps the latter."

"Okay. Good. But first tell me what's going on with your new persuasion."

"Persuasion? That like procedure, Sam?"

"Man."

"Everything is fine."

"Then it's real."

"I think so."

"And the sex is good."

"Very good."

"And you're calm?"

"Well, yes."

"And there's no problem?"

"There is Tony Basillio."

"He ain't a problem, honey. He's a long-term liability. Dump him."

I didn't answer.

"But you look good, doll."

"Well, thank you."

"You got that kind of lilt, Nestleton. Did anyone ever tell you what a knockout you are?"

"Not recently, Sam."

We waited for the light on Sixth Avenue, still heading west.

"Any further questions on my love life, Tully?"

"Not at this moment."

"Good. Let's get to it."

"I'm listening."

"I want to go back to the beginning, Sam."

"Good idea."

"The driver's license. That knockoff of my license, found in Elias's pocket."

"Okay."

"Why did he take it? Why did he knock it off?"

"Fake ID."

"But for what, Sam? Credit card fraud?"

"He didn't get your credit card . . . did he?"

"No. And obviously my license couldn't be an ID for him. Maybe for Terry Ray—but she's a whole lot younger than I am."

"Nobody really looks hard at the picture, honey."

"So, if it's not a credit card scam . . . what?"

"Hard to figure."

"What about cashing checks?"

"Are you missing any?"

"No."

"Your photo ID won't help them unless they have your check."

"You're right, Sam."

We walked on. I was fastening furiously on my thoughts, I was ripping the problem apart. I was attacking like the proverbial Cat Woman.

At the corner of Spring and Varick I hit upon a most peculiar revelation. I offered it up.

"Sam, consider this: A man with no driver's license or credit cards. A woman with no driver's license or credit cards. They want to rent a car together. And they want to hide the fact that they are renting it."

"I'm all ears, honey."

"The man steals two objects—a credit card from Smith and a driver's license from Jones. He presents the credit card to the rental company. They ask for a driver's license. He says he's not driving; his girlfriend will be doing the driving. And besides, he intends to pay in cash when he brings the car back. Then the woman presents a driver's license, which is acceptable because, as you noted, no one looks too closely at those photos. The couple is given the car."

"Dazzling, Nestleton, dazzling. You would make a helluva bad guy. Of course, that kind of scam won't work all the time."

"Agreed. And the scenario has some other problems."

"Like what?"

"Like it would make 'born again' Elias into a real thief."

"That's true."

"And if he was a real thief, why wouldn't he just steal a car if he needs one that bad?"

"Good point."

"And if he took my card out of my wallet, made a photostat, and then replaced it, why didn't he do the same with my credit card?"

"Too hard to counterfeit a credit card."

"Okay. So why didn't he take both and just replace the license after he photostated it? I mean, it would take me days to notice that my credit card was missing, and even then I would never have suspected him."

"Another good point."

"And why did he need a car that bad?"

"Don't know."

We walked awhile in silence. It was a beautiful day.

"Do you have an alternate scenario, Sam?"

"Not really. But maybe he's not a thief and never rented a car with the license. Maybe he liked to collect photo ID's the way some people collect baseball cards. No offense, honey, but he *was* an actor—and they're a bit weird."

"That's ridiculous, Sam."

"Yeah. Well, I'm not thinking so good. My head is fuzzy. I need sustenance."

"You just had a very large cheese Danish," I reminded him.

He stopped. He smiled. I looked past him. My heart sank. The old man had outfoxed me. He had led me to a bar—the Ear Inn. Not one of his usual sleazy hangouts, but the intent was the same.

"Just a few minutes of your time, Nestleton."

We walked inside. I had been here years before, to attend a dramatic reading. It was that kind of place.

The staff was getting ready for lunch. The bartender was cutting limes.

"Who's buying?" Sam asked.

"You."

We sat on stools at the end of the bar, near the door. There were no other customers.

I ordered a glass of water. The bartender grimaced.

Sam ordered straight whiskey and a bottle of dark ale. Then he lit up a cigarette and purred.

"This walk is good for me, Nestleton. All this give-and-take. In fact, I now believe that I have found the cause of the entity which is crushing these arthritic synapses."

"What entity?"

"Writer's block."

"Tully, can't we hold that for later and get back to the matter at hand? The clock, as we both agree, is ticking."

"Everything dovetails, honey. It's one ball of wax. Now, listen. I figured that in order to spruce Harry up for my new book, to make him kinder and gentler, I have to change his views toward womankind."

"That's for sure."

"He can't visit ladies of the night anymore."

"Good!" I was getting snappish. I wanted to get through this nonsense quickly.

"And he can't pay for sex anymore."

"Even better."

"Right. But what happened was, I started writing about Harry's memories of his affairs with women—not the hookers—the real women. And Harry now has a lot of remorse about those women. I mean, he treated some of them bad.

Anyway, as he's thinking about them . . . eleven of them . . . he suddenly can't remember key attributes of the women."

Sam downed his whiskey.

"You mean, Sam, you can't remember the key attributes of your women."

"Of course. I mean, while writing, I am Bondo and Bondo is me."

"Make up attributes."

"No way. You can fake everything in a book—dialogue, milieu, reactions. But memories gotta be real. You take them full blown and bloody out of your own head and ram them into your character."

"You sound like a method actor, Sam."

"So, listen, honey. The reason for the block is because it has been so long since I had a real affair with a woman, I don't remember what men remember about women."

"I can't help you there, Sam."

"I know that. But your friend can."

"What friend?"

"Your new beau."

"Are you crazy, Sam? You want me to question him about the women he slept with in the past, and what he remembers about them? Intimate details?"

"Yeah. That's about it."

"Forget it, Sam. Totally impossible."

He shrugged, ordered another whiskey, and said, "It's probably for the best. Guys like that can be dangerous."

"Dangerous? What are you talking about?"

"You know guys with only initials, not names. Very dangerous."

"Where did you get that theory?"

"It's no theory, honey. Stone-cold fact. Everyone knows that."

I finally realized that Sam was "giving me the business," as my friend says, and I said harshly, "Finish your drink, Sam. Let's get on with it."

"A minute more, Nestleton, a minute more. All this tussling with speculative truth—you like that phrase, honey?—it makes an old guy like me bone weary."

He chuckled, lit another cigarette, and pointed to the shelf behind the bar.

"You ever try that stuff, honey?"

He was pointing at three tall clay bottles with what seemed to be Asian language characters drawn crudely on the sides.

"What is it?" I asked.

"Sake."

"I've had it once or twice."

"You know, Nestleton, I could never figure out what the hell it is. I mean, some people say it's rice wine. Some people tell me it's a liqueur. Some people tell me it's like plum brandy. Some people say it's just a fermented mash. Some people say it's distilled. Some say serve it hot. Others say, cold. Others like to drink it warm."

He finished his second whiskey and began to laugh at the confusion sake caused in him.

"But honey, whatever it is, it's potent. You don't feel a thing after the first two or three. And then—wham!"

He accentuated his *wham* by slamming his hand down on the top of the bar so hard that the bartender almost jumped out of his apron.

I kept staring at those sake bottles. I suddenly felt weary and stupid. Sam's monologue on the mode of sake production had somehow massaged my brain.

I remembered what Laura Arroyo had told me after the funeral: that Terry Ray had worked in a sake bar on Ninth Street, near Second Avenue.

"Sam," I said, "I have to make a call."

I walked to the pay phone in the rear and dialed the Woburn apartment. A female voice answered.

I didn't bother with an introduction. "Has Frenchy been found?"

The answer came swiftly: "No."

I hung up. My palms were sweating. The clock was still ticking.

* * *

An hour later Sam and I stood leaning over a rail on Ninth Street. We were staring down at a series of garbage-strewn steps which ended at a basement door.

That door was huge, ugly, rusted steel, with what seemed to be a peephole.

"That's it?"

"Yes," I said, pointing to the small wooden panel on the building next to the door. Three Japanese characters were drawn elegantly on the wood. It made for a breathtaking contradiction with the door.

It looks like a bomb shelter," Sam noted.

"Yes. It is grim."

"Or maybe a speakeasy. Or a bordello. Or a fence's warehouse."

"From what I understand, these places try to give the illusion of being illicit. Of course they are not."

"The joint makes me nervous," Sam said.

"So do men with initials."

"Touché, honey."

"What would your Harry Bondo do?"

"Go down and knock on the goddamn door. If a Sumo wrestler answers, just say you're from Con Ed."

We walked down the steps. There was a small buzzer right next to the peephole.

I pushed it. No response. I rang again. Still no response.

"Lean on it, doll, lean on it."

I did, and then, after what seemed to be an eternity, the shutter of the peephole swung open. I saw a face. It was that of a slim young Asian woman.

I said in a loud voice: "I'm looking for an old friend of mine. She used to work here."

The woman behind the door gestured that she could not hear me; then she began to point off somewhere to my left.

"She's telling you to use the intercom," Tully whispered. I found it on the side of the building.

I pushed the intercom button. The woman told me patiently: "We do not open until five P.M."

I substituted for my original fabrication, which she had not heard, another, rather ingenious fabrication. "We need information on a woman who used to work here," I said. "She's vanished. We're worried about her."

The shutter across the peephole slammed closed fast and the door opened slowly.

She was a pretty woman, dressed like she had just walked out of the Gap. The way she stood signaled that there would be no further access for us. Past her shoulder one could see a series of small rooms and cubicles with low tables and plush divans.

"Who is this woman?" she asked, and then, seeing Sam Tully for the first time, broke into an affectionate smile, as if the old odd character were her great-uncle.

"Her name is Terry Ray," I said.

"Yes. She did work here. You say she vanished?"

"It appears so," I said in answer, keeping the fabrication going.

"She quit about a year ago. Everyone liked her. We were all sorry when she left."

"Did you ever meet any of her friends?"

"I don't think so. I don't remember."

"What about her boyfriend—Elias Almodovar?"

"No. That name doesn't sound familiar."

"A short, thin, handsome man. He was an actor."

"No. I don't recall meeting him."

"Is there anything you can tell us about her that might help us find her?"

"Not really."

I slipped out the photo of the comedy team.

"What about her?" I asked, pointing out Rachel Woburn.

"No. I don't know her."

"After Terry quit, did she ever come around to the bar? To have a drink or just to say hello."

"No. And I don't know why. She knew we all liked her very much. But she never showed up again."

"Was there anyone she developed a special relationship with, while she worked here, I mean? Another waitress? Someone in the kitchen maybe?"

"I don't think so."

"You said that you never met her boyfriend. But Terry met him right here."

"I'm not a dating service. And I'm sure a lot of our customers tried to date Terry. As I said, everyone liked her. And she did speak the language."

"You mean she knew all about sake?"

"No. I mean she spoke Japanese."

"Really? Terry spoke Japanese? But she comes from Texas."

"She worked in Japan for a few years as a hostess."

"What kind of hostess?"

"That's a complex question," said the young woman, smiling demurely.

Then she wished us good luck, invited us to visit as customers, and swung the door shut.

Tully and I walked to the corner of Second Avenue and Ninth Street.

"I'm hungry," he announced. We turned into a place called the Telephone Bar and ordered lunch at a small table with a checked table cloth, in the smoking section.

Sam ordered a medium rare bleu cheese burger with a bottle of ale. I ordered fish and chips with a ginger ale.

"So what do we got, honey?" Sam asked expansively.

"Well, we already agreed that a knockoff of my driver's license was used by Elias and Terry for renting a car with the purpose of something nefarious."

"Wait! Did I agree to the term 'nefarious'?"

"By implication, you did, Sam. By default."

"Okay. But what about this Terry Ray?"

"You want the whole file?"

"Sure."

"She has an on-again-off-again Texas accent; she wears wild eye makeup; she spends most of her time in antique clothing stores; she has a thing for bell bottom jeans; she slept with a murdered 'born again' actor twenty years her senior who made a living as a substitute doorman; she worked as a waitress; she probably turned some tricks in Tokyo where she learned the language; she was once part of a comedy team—the partner of a young woman whose parents owned an apartment in the building where Terry's lover worked; this same couple own a cat whose present whereabouts are unknown, but who was once taken care of by yours truly."

"That's a real professional report, Nestleton," Sam noted with admiration.

"But it only *seems* like a lot, Tully. It doesn't tell me what I need to know."

"Face it, honey. You don't really know what you need to know."

"Is that right? How about who murdered Elias? Or the reason my license was lifted and then returned. And who took Frenchy? Oh, I think I know very well what I need to know."

"Take it easy, doll. Tell me about the boyfriend."

"You mean Elias."

"Yeah. You got a file on him too?"

"Not really, Sam. He's dead."

Our drinks arrived and we drank in silence for a while.

Sam's face suddenly lit up.

"What is it?"

"I just had a wild thought."

"I'm listening."

"Imagine the existence of an octopus-like criminal operation, run by this Almodovar and Terry Ray. Imagine the tentacles spanning nations and continents. Imagine the theft of thousands of driver's licenses and the rental of thousands of vehicles. Imagine sophisticated marketing and distribution operations. Imagine, Nestleton, the largest 'moonshine' operation in the world. And the product is . . . sake."

He took a long slug of his ale. "Am I brilliant?"

"Yes, Sam. I believe you are."

"But you don't believe a word I just said."

"No," I said. What I really believed I didn't say: that Sam should not have had that whiskey on Spring Street, at the Ear Inn.

The waiter was approaching, a tray in his hands.

"That's good. I'm hungry," said Sam.

After we finished, over coffee, Sam leaned across the table. "I got something else for you, honey."

"Oh?"

"Another theory."

"I love theories, Sam."

"This one's ugly."

"Go ahead."

"Maybe Almodovar went into the park to rob someone. Maybe he wasn't a victim. Maybe he was the mugger and the real victim fought back."

It was such a simple but strange theory. I really didn't know what to say.

Sam blew smoke.

After the lunch, we parted. Sam turned west on Tenth Street and I walked north on Second Avenue.

The day was growing warm. I sat down in the lovely park on Second Avenue and Sixteenth Street, the one by the old Quaker meeting house.

The morning had started off with such a burst of activity . . . with the promise of discovery, of resolution, of action.

Now, everything was torpid.

On the bench, next to me, sat a nanny; her charge was in a carriage. On the bench across from me sat a snoozing derelict.

Nearby, on the grass, were several young people. They were laughing and speaking in a language I couldn't understand. One of the girls was doing cartwheels.

I closed my eyes and slipped into one of those wonderful daydreams.

My agent had gotten me a regular slot in a new, literate sitcom. I played a jolly witch. The money was coming to me in buckets.

A.G. and I got married. It was a glorious ceremony and there was no rancor. Tony gave the bride away.

I purchased an old loft building on the Bowery, turned the top two floors into a magnificent apartment for A.G. and me, and turned the bottom two floors into theaters which I allowed theater groups to use absolutely free of charge.

For A.G., I rented an uptown office where he could practice. No, not law. I freed him of that burden. Now he could become a full-time criminologist who would be hired, for example, by the Greek government to find out once and for all how and why Alexander the Great died.

The daydream was spinning out of control. Luckily, the sun vanished and thunder could be heard in the distance. The sudden climate change brought me back to reality.

I headed toward the bus on Fourteenth Street. Then the thunder vanished and the sun came out again, so I just kept walking west on Fourteenth.

I stopped for a light on Fourth Avenue. Across the street on the downtown side was a bank with a digital clock. It read two-fifty-nine.

The light turned green. I didn't move. People grumbled and walked around me.

A.G.'s place was only two blocks away.

Dare I? Did I want to? Should I? Yes. Yes. Yes. That's what middle-age love is all about—a kind of desperate spontaneity.

I crossed Fourteenth and headed downtown on Fourth Avenue. I stopped in front of that pay phone catty-corner from his house. It was a phone I knew well by now.

But I hesitated. Why, I didn't know. Maybe I could not stand the idea that there was a possibility he would not invite me up. I knew he was there. I could sense it. Don't ask me how. I could envision him going through those old London illustrations, hot on the track of nothing. Like me. But at least my suspects were, for the most part, still alive.

I stepped away from the phone, took a little walk, then returned. Now I'm acting like a fourteen-year-old, I realized.

I slipped the quarter and a dime into the slot and started to dial.

Then I froze.

A man had come out of A.G.'s apartment building. He walked to the curb and stood there.

It was A.G. But he wasn't dressed in his usual casual style. He was wearing an incredibly expensive, beautifully tailored suit. His shirt was light blue. His tie, a pale yellow silk.

I put the receiver back on the hook. I didn't know what to do.

Suddenly, a cab pulled up near the curb. A.G. didn't get in. Someone got out.

It was a young woman. She was wearing an incredible dress—sheer, flowing, white rayon with all kinds of tie-dyed designs in pink, yellow, and blue. The dress was low-cut, very low-cut, and the sleeves billowy.

A.G. took the woman in his arms and spun her around.

I could see her face: It was Rachel Woburn.

I had to hold on to the side of the pay phone to keep from reeling.

Chapter 11

They stood together near the curb a long time, in their finery, speaking to each other.

I recovered my equilibrium and was flooded with rage. Against him! Against myself! Against the world.

Was the man insane? He had told me in a thousand ways that we were lovers . . . that he was desperately in love with me . . . that I was the best thing that ever happened to him.

And now he was already cheating on me with a child, almost.

They disengaged a bit and walked west on Twelfth Street.

I followed them. I didn't really know why. But I followed them without qualms, staying half a block behind.

They turned south on University Place. I cut the distance between us to a quarter of a block.

I began to feel like a hit woman. I felt that I

had a weapon in my purse and I was, in the popular parlance, going to blow the bastard away. Yes! Alice Nestleton starring in a remake of *La Femme Nikita.* And to think I used to consider myself a classically trained actress. Ah Love, thou art grim.

They turned west on Ninth Street. That, I knew, was a long block; I could keep them in view, easily. I slowed down a bit.

When I turned the corner, they were gone.

Where? There was a bus stop. Had they jumped on a bus? No. There was no bus anywhere in sight.

Had they crossed the street and gone into the doorman building? Possible. But why? She didn't live there.

I continued west on Ninth, walking slowly, confused.

Then I saw the Italian restaurant, a small, expensive-looking place named La Bella Causa.

I had noticed it in the past, but I had never eaten there.

I peered in. The front was empty, but the garden was open and I could see people milling about back there . . . well-dressed people.

There was a band. There were waiters moving about with trays. It was obviously a cocktail party or reception of some sort.

The bar in the front area was open to the public. I slipped in and sat down. I ordered a Campari and soda.

From where I sat I could see them. A.G. and Rachel were standing side by side, touching lightly, sipping wine.

A.G. looked very happy. Rachel was swaying slightly to the music.

I lay my head down on the top of the bar and started to cry. The bartender approached and leaned over toward me solicitously. I paid and rushed out.

An hour later I was home. I have no idea what route I took or why it took me so long.

Once home I sat on my bed and stared out of the window, oblivious to everything.

Bushy came up beside me. Pancho sat ten feet away and stared at us.

A long time passed. No one moved. It began to rain outside. Soon I realized we were all staring at one another.

And the idea of a jilted woman and two cats mourning together on a rainy June afternoon in this manner was just too ridiculous.

I shooed Bushy and Pancho away, started to laugh, started to cry, started to pace.

I worked myself up into a monumental rage, cursing A.G. and his progeny, and smashing two beautiful teacups to smithereens as I moved from one end of the loft to another like a lioness.

Then I collapsed onto the sofa. I couldn't sleep. I couldn't not sleep. I found myself slipping into a depression.

My body felt heavy, very heavy. There was a slow pounding in my temples and I could not focus on anything.

The loft grew dark. I literally watched my illuminated clock hand move. Minute by minute, hour by hour, dumbly.

The phone rang at nine-thirty. I picked it up.

"Nestleton?"

"Yes?"

"It's me, Tully. Did I wake you up?"

"No."

"I just wanted to find out if you came up with anything."

"About what?"

"About Terry Ray and her Japanese adventure."

"No."

"You sound funny. What's the matter, doll?"

I didn't answer.

"Nestleton! You there?"

"Yes."

"What's going on?"

"Nothing."

"You sound terrible. Are you sick?"

"No."

"Something happened, honey. I can feel it. Tell me what happened."

I did not want to talk anymore. But I didn't want to hang up.

"Is it something with the case? Did that Frenchy the cat get hurt?"

"No."

"Where'd you go after we split?"

"Nowhere, Sam."

"You're lying to me."

I didn't answer. Then I heard him curse a blue streak.

"You want to see him, didn't you?"

I didn't answer.

"And something blew up in your face, didn't it?"

I didn't answer.

"He dumped you!"

I didn't answer.

"Look, honey, I need a cup of coffee. Good coffee. You going to make me a cup?"

I didn't answer. He hung up the phone. I couldn't move. It never dawned on me he would really come over at this time of night to get a cup of coffee. But I didn't really care one way or the other.

The bell rang at 10 P.M. He arrived with coffee and pizza.

"Nestleton," he said, "you sounded like you

couldn't even boil water. So I got you some Starbuck's Kenya brew and a broccoli pizza, because I know you're a health-food nut."

I sat back down on the sofa. He pulled a chair over and began to attack the pizza, looking up at me from time to time. He finished two slices, discarding the broccoli, and then started on the coffee.

"You suicidal, honey?"

"No."

"You want me to call Tony?"

"No."

"Your niece? Or that friend of yours—Nora?"

"No."

"You going to tell me what happened? Or do I have to beat it out of you?"

I told him what had happened.

When I had finished my softspoken monotone of a narrative, he didn't say a word for a long time. He slurped his coffee and smoked a cigarette. The open pizza box on the floor drew Bushy and Pancho's rapt attention.

Finally, he pulled out a deck of cards from his back pocket. "You play Casino?"

"I used to."

He dragged a small table over and started to deal the cards.

After they were dealt, he took out a bottle,

shook loose two pills, and handed them to me with the other container of coffee.

"Swallow them, Nestleton."

"What are they?"

"Sleeping pills from south of the border."

I took the pills and swallowed them. It wasn't time to be choosy.

He grinned. "I did warn you about guys with initials, didn't I?"

"Yes, that you did, Sam."

We began to play. It was very sweet of him to come over . . . to be worrying about me . . . to bring me some comfort.

I played but I didn't know what I was doing. My eyelids began to close.

"Go on to bed, honey," Sam said. "I'll camp out on the couch."

"You don't have to stay over, Sam. I'm not going to do anything foolish. I'm fine, really."

"Sure you are, Nestleton. You look as fine as a car bomb with an exposed trip wire that's about to be stepped on by a cow."

And so I went to bed. I was asleep in minutes.

Morning came. I sat up. Who was that strange man boiling water in my kitchen? Where were my cats? And why weren't they screaming for their breakfast?

The sun was pouring in. Then I saw Bushy

and Pancho calmly eating their morning meal. Except their bowls were not in the usual place.

Everything came into focus.

"I fed the brutes," Sam Tully announced, "and now I'm making you coffee. I ask you, honey, am I not the best houseguest you ever had?"

I showered and put on tennis shoes and a rust-colored jumpsuit I had purchased at the St. Luke's Church thrift shop. I left my hair loose.

"You need a new toaster," Sam declared as we sat down to breakfast.

He had overbuttered the slices of toast, which lay between bookends of jagged tomato slices.

There was a large serving spoon protruding from a jar of imported jam that I had received as a Christmas gift.

"You look better than you did last night, doll."

"I feel better."

"Remember what Harry Bondo said—I think it was in the second book: 'Heartbreak is like poison sumac. It doesn't matter how you treat it or don't treat it, it clears up in three days.' "

I smiled and sipped the coffee. It tasted quite good.

"You like it?"

"Not bad, Sam."

"Yeah, I got the touch. Actually I used a little

of that coffee I brought in last night, mixed it with your instant espresso, and added a bit of salt."

"Salt? In coffee?"

"Yeah. It's one of my secrets."

"Sometimes you astonish me, Sam."

"Only because you forget who I am."

"Oh? And who are you?"

"Just an old hippie. A bit hard on the outside. But all kinds of peace and love and salt on the inside—like Gandhi."

I laughed. "You're right. I never thought of you that way, as a geriatric hippie."

"Sure. Of course I didn't become a hippie until I was fifty. You know me, honey, always slow on the uptake."

"Just the word 'hippie' always brings back nice memories to me, Sam. When I finally got to New York to study acting, in the early 1970s, the hippies were on their last legs. But I used to see them in the park."

"You mean Central Park?"

"Yes. In fact, the first week I was in New York, I stumbled on a hippie wedding."

I spread some jam on my toast, smiling at the memory.

"Was it wild? Headbands? Tambourines?"

"No. Not wild at all, Sam. Charming. Guitars, not tambourines. Five couples were getting married. The women in tie-dyed see-through wedding dresses. The men in stovepipe hats, bare feet, and old army dress jackets. The preacher was so stoned he didn't know which way to face."

"Damn! I haven't seen a see-through dress in a long time. They always made me uncomfortable."

Right there and then I was hit by such a powerful coincidence that I burst into an almost hysterical laugh.

"What's the matter with you?" Tully asked.

"Sam, listen to me. The dress she was wearing yesterday was the same kind of dress I saw in the park in 1972."

"This 'she' you're talking about . . . you mean Rachel Whatshername?"

"Yes! Yes!"

I stood up. "Sam, remember I told you about a fire at the gallery that was mounting Bea Woburn's show?"

"Yeah."

"And where the fire started?"

"In the next building, you said. A robbery at a sweatshop. Owned by Hong Kong people."

"Right. Do you remember what I said they manufactured?"

"Wedding dresses."

* * *

An hour later we stood by the curb on Bond Street, next to a dumpster filled with fire debris that should have already been towed away.

There were no repairs or new construction going on at the Patroclus Gallery this morning. A security screen was in place around the front entrance. On the ground floor of the adjoining building, where the robbery had taken place, was a dingy but very deep office furniture store.

"Let me handle this," Sam said. "You're too wound up."

We walked inside. Several young men were moving huge desks on dollies. A white-haired man seemed to be supervising. His name, we learned, was Walter Tolkin. And he was the owner of the store.

Sam introduced us as reporters from the *Bowery News,* a neighborhood newspaper.

We were there, Sam announced, to find out more about the fire, which, he added, many people in the neighborhood considered "fishy."

And to find out why the dumpster had not been pulled away.

"I never heard of the *Bowery News,*" Tolkin said.

"We're a new publication," Sam told him.

"I've complained about that dumpster. Nothing happened."

"What was the name of that Hong Kong firm where the fire started?"

"My My Fashions."

"Do you know how I can find them?"

"I hear they're gone. The foreman stops by every once in a while. Trying to salvage the sewing machines, I guess. But the owners are in Hong Kong. By the way, if you people are reporters, how come you don't take notes?"

"You're old-fashioned, Mr. Tolkin," Sam noted smugly.

"I guess I am."

"Can you explain the fire?"

"What do you mean, 'explain' it? The cops said it was B&E. The thieves tried to cut open a safe with a torch. The sparks ignited the fabric lying around the place."

"But the fire didn't touch your place."

"Well, no it didn't. Instead of moving down or up, the fire moved across the air shaft between the buildings, and to that gallery on the ground floor. I was damn lucky. Lot of wood in here. It would have been a tinderbox."

"Isn't it peculiar to have a fire like that jump across the air shaft?"

"Maybe. Maybe not. I wouldn't know."

Sam nodded slowly, as if Walter Tolkin had said something profound. The proprietor kept staring at me, wondering, I suppose, why I hadn't said a word. Maybe he thought I was a cub reporter.

"You said something about a foreman."

Mr. Tolkin shrugged. "Foreman, manager, slave driver, whatever. I don't know his title. But I do know he's out of a job now."

"You said he still comes around."

"Right. In fact, he stopped in about two hours ago."

"What's his name?"

"Johnny Chung."

"Do you have a telephone number where we can reach him?"

"I don't know his number. But when he isn't working, he's in that poolroom on Houston and Mott."

Then Tolkin asked when we'd be taking the picture of him that would accompany the story in the *Bowery News.* Sam told him the staff photographer would be in later.

We didn't have any trouble at all finding Johnny Chung in that rather upscale poolroom at Houston and Mott.

He was the only individual there over the age of twenty-five. And he wasn't playing pool. He was seated in a small lounge in front of one of seven TV sets, watching some kind of exotic athletic event featuring strong men who race with huge barrels on their shoulders.

Because Sam had done so well in that office furniture store, he continued in his reporter guise, and I continued to remain silent.

As for Johnny Chung, he was a short, thickset man with a baseball cap and a bandage over the bridge of his nose.

He quickly admitted that he was indeed the Johnny Chung who ran the shop for the Hong Kong people. He, too, had never heard of the *Bowery News,* but he seemed, like Mr. Tolkin, to talk as if he had nothing at all to hide.

Sam knew intuitively what I wanted. He knew what I wanted to know . . . And he went for the jugular.

"What was in the safe?" he asked.

"What safe?" Chung replied, his eyes glued to the TV set.

"The safe the thieves were trying to open when it all lit up."

"Don't know a thing about safes, Pops. I'm a floor man. I run the girls and the machines. What's in the office is not my business."

"So what got burned up?"

"You mean stock?"

"Yeah."

"About three hundred garments. Most of them returns. Come mid-June, the stores start shipping back a lot of the spring line that was on consignment."

"What kind of stuff did My My Fashions put out?"

"Knockoffs."

"Of what?"

"This year . . . sixties stuff . . . retro gear . . . hippie wedding dresses. Big in London and on the West Coast. Tie up the bottoms and wear them over high boots. 'Funky and fey,' said English *Vogue.* 'Nineteen ninety-eight becomes nineteen sixty-eight.' "

Sam looked at me. I felt my whole body tingling.

I whispered in his ear: "Try to get a price, Sam."

"That a budget line?" Sam asked Chung.

"Hell no. Fifteen to seventeen hundred bucks apiece."

"What happens to My My now? Rebuild? Relocate? What?"

Chung laughed good-naturedly, shifting his hat, keeping his eyes on the screen. "You can't ever figure Hong Kong people," he said.

Ten minutes later we were seated in a bar on Great Jones Street. To my astonishment, I blurted out that I wanted a bottle of ale. Sam ordered whiskey. The place had just opened. I was so agitated. I could hardly sit.

"You were brilliant, Sam. Absolutely brilliant."

"Glad to be of assistance, honey."

"Assistance? Oh no, Sam! Not just assistance. You put the nail in the coffin."

"Whose coffin?"

"A.G. Roth's. Listen, Sam, I know what happened. I know now. I see the contours."

"That's nice. I don't see a damn thing."

"Listen!" I grabbed the ale bottle as the bartender was placing it down and took a long, quite unladylike slug of it.

Sam stared into his whiskey and lit a cigarette.

"Are you listening, Sam?"

"How many times are you going to ask me that?"

I poured some ale into the glass and sipped it gently.

"Imagine the lovers, Sam. Nothing special—right? Just a typical May-December affair. Rachel, the young woman. A.G. Roth, the older man.

"But it's really not typical, Sam. These lovers share a few very profound characteristics. For one, they are both very unhappy with what they do. A.G. doesn't want to be a lawyer. Rachel doesn't want to be a comedienne.

"Second, they are both in trouble financially—always behind the eight ball; in one way or another being subsidized by the Woburns. In fact, neither of them can make a living.

"And third, they know a lot of people in common . . . Are you with me, Sam?"

"I'm with you, honey."

"Good. Because now it gets interesting. A.G. Roth is Bea Woburn's lawyer. So he knows all about that art show, 'Mind and Material.' He probably was at that gallery many times. So, while there, he learns all about My My Fashions and their dresses. He tells Rachel about them. She contacts the Pink Hippo, using Terry Ray as an introduction. Arlene Boccio tells her the dresses are worth money. Rachel and A.G. plan the robbery. They contact Elias, again using an innocent Terry Ray as a reference. Elias steals my license and rents a van.

"Now it comes time for action. A.G. and Rachel steal the dresses. They fire the place to cover their tracks. Rachel, in a fit of hatred for her parents, torches the gallery on the way out. After the robbery, born-again Elias becomes remorseful, threatening to go to the police. A.G. murders him, or has him murdered.

"And the lovers live happily ever after in the sure knowledge that they have both finally found paying trades—as thieves and murderers."

I expected Sam to react with enthusiasm to my map of the conspiracy. He didn't. In fact, he looked a bit dour.

"What's the matter?" I asked.

"A few things. What about the dresses? And what about the cat?"

"I think the dresses are buried somewhere until things cool down. Maybe a few are in circulation now. I know Rachel was wearing one when I saw her. But I think Miss Boccio won't try to move them until next spring.

"And the cat . . . I don't know, Sam. It has to be some kind of threat or warning. But to whom and why it is directed, I don't know. Wait! It has to be directed at either Sidney or Beatrice Woburn, I guess. They're the ones who love Frenchy."

"Are you sure A.G. killed Elias?"

"Maybe not with his own hands . . . but he is responsible."

"You sure?"

"It's all there, Sam. In black and white."

He laughed. I became infuriated. "What is so funny?"

"Like always, honey, you craft a beautiful quilt. But this one is made of chocolate. A little heat and the pattern melts. To be honest, Nestleton, I really wouldn't advise you trying to sell that quilt to the NYPD."

"Okay, Sam. Forget the chocolate imagery. Where's the flaw in my story? Where's the illogic?"

"Don't get me wrong. The tale you spun is logical. The problem is motive."

"Whose motive?"

"Yours."

"My motive is always the same—to find the truth of what happened."

"The guy cheated on you. He broke your heart. You might be making him the bad guy because you hate his guts now. This A.G. might be a two-timing bastard, but you have no real proof that he's a thief and a murderer. Not real proof, honey. Not one lousy thumbprint. Right?"

"Sometimes, Sam, the logic is so strong, it becomes the proof."

"Tell me, honey. Your Tony has all kinds of adventures with young actresses and you laugh it off. This A.G. makes one slip and you go around the bend. Is there any logic to that?"

I did not wish to discuss that paradox, which was surely true. I didn't answer Sam. I drank more ale. Sam drank more whiskey.

"You know what I think?" Tully asked.

"What?"

"I have to get home and see what Pickles is doing."

"Yes, you should."

"I'm lying. I'm not thinking about Pickles. I'm thinking about you . . . about telling you something. Want to hear it? Want to hear some ugly truths from an old man?"

"Sure, Sam. I'm ready."

"You acted like you were resisting with that lawyer guy. But in fact, you pushed it. You jumped into his bed. You were so hungry for love, it was like you were wearing a badge."

I poured the last of my ale into the glass with a flourish.

"And I thought, Sam, that you would help me bring in the head of A.G. Roth."

"I will if he's guilty."

"There's only one way to find out, Sam."

"How's that?"

"Tempt him. Flush him out. Make him commit himself."

Sam laughed wickedly. "But you already did that, honey, and look where it got you."

"I mean, force him out of his innocence. Make the bait so tempting he has to act."

"You mean frighten him, don't you?"

"Okay. Frighten him."

"I'm listening, honey, but I have to get home for Pickles. Why don't you just hold on to your plan for a while. I'm sure it's a doozy."

We walked back to his Spring Street apartment. As we did, I constructed a wolf trap in my mind's eye, fully aware that it would be impossible to follow Humane Society rules regarding the trapping of predators.

I stared down at the old, ugly portable typewriter. Sam was messing with the cat's bowls, filling them with various kinds of food.

"He's on the roof," Sam said, speaking of Pickles. "He doesn't like coming down during nice weather."

Sam started rattling spoons and cans to entice the spotted cat down. He stuck his head out the window and looked up. "There's no sign of him. He must be hunting."

"Why don't you get one of those sweet little laptop things, Sam. This machine you work on is a monstrosity.

He positioned the cat's bowls just inside the kitchen door; then he joined me by the typewriter.

"The problem is," he explained, "I am at least two technologies behind. I never made it to electric typewriters, much less electronic ones. So now I'm too old to make the leap to word processors. And besides, I pound the keys. Hard. I'd bust one of those laptops to pieces."

I shrugged. "To each his own," I said.

"You want something to eat, doll?"

"No."

"Tea? Coffee?"

"No. Just a few sheets of white paper and a pencil."

He provided these. I sat down at his "desk" and proceeded to work for a hard fifteen minutes.

Then I handed a sheet of paper to him—on his easy chair.

"What is this?"

"What does it look like?"

"A drawing of a dress."

"Correct. The dress Rachel was wearing. The kind of dress My My produced this spring."

"So what do I do with it?"

"Tomorrow morning, late in the morning, you take it into the Pink Hippo. Ask for Arlene Boccio. Show it to her. Tell her you have a great many of these dresses to sell. You want to get rid of them fast. You'll give her a good price."

"And what is she going to do?"

"Here's what I think she'll do: First, turn pale. Then question you about where you got them. You'll say nothing. She'll say she has to think on it; but either way she'll want to see the dresses themselves, in the flesh, so to speak. You'll leave your phone number and walk out. She'll call A.G. Roth and give him hell. She'll think she's been double-crossed. A.G. will swear their dresses are still safely hidden. He'll offer to check out your story. He'll call you and set up an appointment to inspect the merchandise."

"Then what?"

"You'll meet him. The minute he says he's ready to pay cash for them and you open a suitcase stuffed with newspapers, I shut the trap on his foot."

"You're starting to sound like a bounty hunter, Nestleton."

"One important thing, Sam. You have to wear a wire all the time. From the moment you walk into the Pink Hippo. Oh, not a real wire. Just one of those minirecorders. They're twenty dollars. I think you can hook it right on your belt, like a beeper. In fact, it looks like a beeper. Record everything, Sam. Keep it running. You have the twenty dollars?"

"Yeah. I'll get one this afternoon. Where do I meet this A.G.?"

"I'll leave that up to you. But it should be someplace with booths. Make the appointment for four-thirty in the afternoon. I'll get to the place at four-forty-five. I'll wait outside. The minute he makes a cash offer, the minute he wants to see the merchandise, you go to the bathroom. I'll see you go from the outside. That's the signal. When you come back to the booth, I'll come in."

"And nail him."

"Exactly."

"Honey, you really want this creep, don't you?"

I didn't respond to that particular question. "So, here it is again, in a nutshell, Sam. Just before noon, you visit Boccio with the drawing and the wire. You call me the minute you get home. You wait for A.G.'s call. You set up the meeting. You call me to confirm. You go to the meeting. When it's time to move, you signal me by going to the bathroom."

"Got it. Now, where do I meet him again?"

"You tell me."

"How about that bar, the Old Town, on Eighteenth Street?"

"Why always a bar, Sam?"

"Because only bars have booths. And Old Town has beauties. You don't want it in a bar, Nestleton? Fine. You tell me where to meet him."

"All right, all right. The Old Town," I conceded. I was too wound up to think of alternatives. And everyone knows that nefarious, clandestine meetings with at least one known criminal present have to take place in a booth. Besides, A.G. lived only seven or eight blocks away from that particular bar.

Pickles then popped his face into the open window.

"Look! The beast in the rooftop jungle," yelled Sam.

I stared at Pickles. He reminded me that on my way home I must stop in a church and light a candle for Frenchy.

As I left, Sam called out: "What if Rachel calls me after the visit to the Pink Hippo?"

"I don't think she will, Tully. But go ahead and meet with whoever wants to meet with you."

"You can count on me, honey. I'll be witty, web-footed, and wired."

Chapter 12

I woke at six in the morning and fed the cats. Bushy, suspicious of the early hour, inspected the contents of each of his three bowls minutely—regular canned cat food in dish one, the hard, pebbly variety in number two, and finally, his water bowl—before commencing.

Pancho, on the other hand, seemed happy at the early hour breakfast, and indulged in one of his favorite pastimes: flicking the dry food out of the bowl and into the water dish, then retrieving the sodden orbs.

At seven o'clock I called Sam to make sure he was up. He was grumpy during the necessary interrogation.

Did he purchase the minirecorder? And the cassette to load it?

Did he remember the address of the Pink Hippo?

Did he have a suitcase and newspaper to stuff in it?

Did he have my drawing?

Everything seemed in order.

"What should I wear?" he asked after the interrogation.

"Well, Sam, something a little more upscale than your usual derelict chic."

"Derelict chic? Is that my style? No wonder people keep trying to interview me on the street."

There was silence on the phone.

Then: "How about suspenders?"

"Sounds fine."

"And maybe my funeral shoes."

"What are those?"

"Exactly what they sound like. A pair of shoes I save to wear to funerals."

"But you're not going to a funeral, Sam."

"True but trivial, honey. I'll think on it."

I hung up and made coffee. Then I sat down and began to pay bills, or at least look them over.

At nine o'clock the phone rang. I picked it up immediately, figuring it was Sam.

No. Not Sam Tully. It was Tony Basillio.

So shocked was I at hearing his voice that my eyes darted about the loft, as if seeking an open window for me to fly out of.

"You thought I was dead, Swede?"

I didn't want to talk to Tony. Maybe it was because of guilt. Maybe something else.

"Can I get back to you, Tony?"

"Someone's there?"

"No, no. Nothing like that."

"You in trouble?"

"No."

"You miss me?"

"Of course I do."

"Call me later," he said, and hung up.

At nine-thirty I was finished with my bills. I called Tully. He was typing. Yes, he said, he was ready to go. Yes, he would leave around eleven.

I made myself a pathetic grilled cheese sandwich. Then I sat down with an old Gertrude Stein anthology and read in a desultory fashion about her lack of adventure during the German occupation of France in World War II.

At eleven I put the book down and started to pace.

From time to time I stopped in front of the mirror. As one gets older, it's more and more difficult to recognize oneself in the reflected image.

But there was no doubt I was verging on the dowdy.

I shook my hair out. Surely I was no longer

the tall, thin, very pretty young farm girl with the white-gold hair.

What had that critic said of me? "Don't be fooled. She may look like a dumb showgirl from the sticks—but this lady can act."

The phone didn't ring until twelve-thirty.

It was Sam.

"Okay. I'm home," he said. He was breathing heavily.

"What happened?"

"You were dead right, Nestleton. She turned five shades of pale when I showed her that drawing. Then she wanted to know if the merchandise was hot. Then she said she doesn't touch that kind of stuff. Then she wanted me to quote her a price. Then she said she wanted to see the stuff. She was getting real flustered. Finally she took a deep breath and said I should leave my number and get out. She'd contact me soon, she said—very soon."

"Excellent, Sam, excellent."

"Yeah, I thought I pulled it off kind of brilliantly."

"Now we go to Act Two."

He laughed and hung up.

I sat down and picked up Gertrude Stein again. This time I didn't even try to read.

At one-twenty the phone rang again. It was Sam.

"He called."

"A.G.?"

"I guess it was him. Low, kind of gentle voice."

"That's him."

"All he said was he wants to see the dresses. No names. I told him to meet me in Old Town at four-thirty. At a booth."

"And?"

"And he wanted to know what I look like. I told him I look like Charlton Heston if he had been buried for eight months."

"And?"

"He hung up. You know, I kinda like his voice, honey, but he seems a bit young."

"You know me, Sam. I like 'em vigorous and criminal," I quipped. My voice, alas, was filled with bitterness.

"Act Three—right, Nestleton?"

"Act Three, Sam."

How did I spend the next few hours? I don't really recall. I did have, for some reason, a rural fantasy, though. My cats and I were ensconced in a lovely cottage. Don't ask me where. In the late afternoon the three of us would don straw hats, wide-brimmed ones, and repair to a magnificent garden.

I left my loft at three-thirty and walked slowly uptown. Stately. I carried no purse.

The June breeze was delightful. I turned east on Fourteenth Street and browsed among the cut-rate clothing stalls.

My calmness was uncanny. I wasn't acting like an avenging angel, but there was no doubt I was one. A.G. Roth was about to pay for his crimes: murder and betrayal and God knew what else.

I could have, perhaps should have, brayed like one of those tough, brassy blond cabaret singers in those tough old movies, standing over her man after she has drilled two holes in his head: "You see what you get when you two-time Mabel."

I winced at that particular flight of imagination.

I checked the time—4:15 P.M. I turned north on Fifth Avenue and window-shopped for a bit.

The Armani store, as usual, fascinated me. I have never even known a man who wore an Armani. (And I was in the theater.) Shouldn't I have known one? Why did I intuitively dislike men who wore Armani suits? I didn't dislike women who wore Chanel suits.

I paused and dawdled at Eighteenth Street. It was now four-thirty. If everything was going as planned, they were both inside the bar now, in a booth.

I headed east walking slowly, very slowly. My

heart was starting to pound and I felt that funny kind of tightening in my neck. Yes, I had to go very slowly.

At precisely four-forty-five I reached the large plate glass window of the Old Town Bar.

I looked inside. The long bar was almost empty.

The booths lined the wall opposite the bar.

Faces and bodies in the booths could not be clearly seen from the window.

All I could see were legs. Two of the booths had only one pair of legs.

One, close to the door, had two pairs of legs, facing each other under the table.

Then I saw the ugly old valise, on the floor, beside a leg.

I stepped back. Even though I was looking for it. The object frightened me. I looked again. It had to be Sam's valise. It was too ugly not to be his—too battered.

Now I had to watch carefully. I had to wait for the sign.

I moved to one side of the window and kept my eyes glued to the suitcase.

Nothing happened. Now, Sam! Now! I kept whispering to myself.

Then I saw him stand up, move to the aisle, stare out toward the street for a moment, turn and walk to the men's room in the rear.

I pressed my face against the window like a kid watching a circus she couldn't afford to enter.

He wasn't in there long. He headed back toward the booth. Yes, he was wearing red suspenders.

With a kind of glee I pushed open the door and strode in, timing my stride to meet Sam at the booth.

He slid in.

I stared at the seated A.G. Roth.

Only, it wasn't Roth.

Seated across from Sam was a slim young man in a suit and tie. I had never seen him before in my life.

The stranger spat out words in a hoarse, frightened whisper. "What's going on here? Who is she?"

Sam didn't reply.

The young man stood up and tried to move out of the booth.

I sat down beside him, heavily, blocking his exit.

Slowly, he took his seat again.

My head was spinning. "Who are you?" I asked, just as he had asked Tully about me.

The man didn't answer.

"What is your relationship to Arlene Boccio?"

No answer.

"Do you know A.G. Roth?"

No answer.

Suddenly Sam reached across the table, so quick for an old man, and slipped his hand into the pocket of the stranger's suit—the inside breast pocket.

He pulled out a billfold and slammed it down onto the table.

I flipped it open.

It was difficult to believe. There were four pieces of ready identification in that billfold and all identified the carrier as Anton Woburn; the man-child of Beatrice and Sidney that I had heard mentioned briefly.

"Were you the one who gave the dress to Rachel?"

He didn't say anything. He had folded his arms. His thin body was rigid, his eyes straight ahead, looking past Sam, at the booth partition.

I could see the facial similarity with his father.

We were all trapped in that booth. We could neither fight nor flee.

It was the kind of situation where one either does nothing at all or does something very daring.

Luckily, I opted for the latter.

"Sam, give me the recorder."

Sam plucked the little machine off his belt and placed it beside Anton's billfold. It did indeed look like a beeper. The audiocassette within was virtually invisible from the outside.

I picked it up and held it in front of Anton's face. "Don't you understand?" I said. "Arlene Boccio set you up. She's helping us roll up the organization. We have no dresses to sell."

His eyes quickly turned toward me. "Are you cops?" he whispered.

I didn't answer his question. I rolled the recorder in my fingers, setting up the fabrication a bit dramatically. "And do you know what's on this tape, Anton Woburn? Arlene Boccio's statement that you murdered Elias Almodovar."

"You're lying," he said.

"No. No. It's on here. You knifed him to death. You faked a mugging and knifed him to death. In Central Park. Arlene spelled it out for us. Every gory detail. How Elias could not abide being a thief anymore. How he wanted to confess to God, to the police, to everyone. It's all here."

He was silent. I kept it up. "Robbery is not too bad, Anton. And arson is only a little worse. But for the murder of Elias Almodovar, you'll never get out of prison. That is where you're going to die."

He buried his face in his hands. Sam drank some whiskey. He seemed to have compassion for the young man. He seemed to dislike my thuggish approach. Did he have an alternative?

Then, suddenly, he bolted upright, his back ramrod straight. He pressed back against the partition and closed his eyes. His right hand began to nervously rub his cheek.

"Of course she'd tell you it was me who killed that fool. She's protecting her friend. But it was Terry Ray who killed him. It was Terry Ray who couldn't control him anymore. He was getting drunk on God and full of remorse. I didn't even know Elias. I met him only once, during the robbery. He drove the van."

The young man had fallen hook, line, and sinker for the recorder ruse, had even admitted the robbery. He was scared.

Sam leaned across the table and started to play with the billfold.

"You know what I really don't understand? Why all the murder and mayhem for a few lousy dresses that you really don't know if you can sell?"

"The dresses," Anton said, "were a finder's fee for Arlene. That's all."

"A finder's fee?"

"Yes. The real money was in the jeans."

Sam and I stared at each other, totally perplexed.

"What jeans, Anton? What are you talking about?"

"In my mother's show, you know, the one called 'Mind and Material,' at that Bond Street gallery—there was an exhibitor named Wolff. I forget his first name. He had done a huge crazy collage. One whole wall.

"The theme was jeans and pop culture. There must have been thirty pairs of jeans hanging up there, along with records, cans, bottles, shoes, and old newspaper headlines.

"Wolff comes from Colorado. Old mining country. He picked up a lot of the jeans in junk stores. What he didn't know was that about fifteen of them dated from about 1900."

He paused, drank some beer, and then continued. Nothing could stop him now. He was in the confessional mode.

"They were authentic miners' Levi's of the era, with a leather patch on the belt and one back pocket. They were cut by hand and made from very heavy denim. It was Arlene Boccio who noticed them during a preview of the show."

"What was she doing there?"

"My mother had sent out invitations to Rachel's old friends and associates. Terry got the invite. She took Arlene Boccio. When she saw the jeans hanging up on the wall, she told Terry they were probably worth fifty thousand dollars each. From collectors in Japan. For some reason the Japanese go crazy over old denims.

"Terry was interested. She knew Japan. She'd lived there. And she knew I needed money. The My My Fashions place was the weirdest of coincidences. It was next door to the gallery and Arlene always loved their knockoffs.

"So that was the way we did the split. I got forty percent of the jeans money. Terry got forty percent, and out of that she paid Elias. Arlene got twenty percent and all the dresses.

"Terry and I did the break-in. It was easy. We stole the dresses and the jeans. We torched both places. It made sense. I went to Japan with the jeans. Terry made the contacts for me by phone. I got the money—not as much as we thought it would be, thirty thousand each—and came back. The dresses are in a ministorage place in Hoboken.

"That's why Arlene panicked when she saw the drawing. She thought Terry and I were double-crossing her—selling the dresses that were part of her cut."

He was sweating now and he had talked so fast that his words had tumbled over each other.

"Was A.G. Roth in on this?"

"You mean my mother's lawyer?"

"Yes."

"No, of course not. I wouldn't use him to take out the garbage."

"Your sister—was she involved?"

"No. Not at all."

"Why did you take Frenchy?"

"The 'mechanicals.' "

"The what?"

"The 'mechanicals.' The 'blues.' The compositor's original of the show's exhibit catalog. We burned everything up at the gallery—catalogs, art works, everything. We planned it that way so that no one would know we were just after a single piece . . . so that everyone would think there was only one robbery that night at My My.

"But then we found out that the gallery had used my father's firm to print the descriptive catalog. And I knew his firm always saved the 'blues.' So I put on a silly wig and a dress and just walked in and took Frenchy, leaving an alley cat to rub it in.

"I put Frenchy in a boarding kennel. Then Terry made an anonymous call to my father. We'd trade the cat for the 'mechanicals' of the catalog. Father said he couldn't find them. He was looking for them, he said. Of course, maybe he hates my mother so much now that he's happy the cat was taken."

"How much did you net from the jeans sale in Japan?" Sam asked.

"I could only sell twelve pair."

"That's close to four hundred thousand!" Sam noted in wonderment. He looked at me. "And to think I bought this kid a beer."

"Where is this kennel?" I asked Anton.

"Thirty-first and Ninth."

For some reason, I was now, like Sam, beginning to develop a grudging compassion for this young man. He seemed alternately proud and contrite; intelligent and dim-witted; careful and careless; criminal and innocent.

As for me, I was, I suppose, bemused at how close I had been to the actual workings of the criminal enterprise—but so far from the truth of it all.

As for the jeans? I could not even begin to speculate on a pair of old rough-cut denim trousers transported across the Pacific to someone in Japan who would pay thirty thousand dollars cash for the privilege of staring at it, in perpetuity.

I slipped the card containing Detective Sofia Little's number across the table to Sam.

"Will you make the call?" I asked.

He groaned, slid out from the booth, and headed toward the pay phone.

"What will they do to me?" Anton asked.

"I don't know."

"What should I do?"

"I don't know. But you need a lawyer."

He burst out in a kind of maniacal laughter. "Maybe I'll get two. My mother's lawyer and my father's lawyer."

"Maybe," I said, "you ought to send your mother flowers."

My suggestion poisoned the atmosphere. We sat in silence until Tully returned. Then I walked out.

I didn't go straight from the Old Town to the kennel on Thirty-first Street. Oh, I did head purposefully toward the kennel. But halfway there, at about Twenty-third and Ninth, I developed a ravenous hunger.

Maybe it was my own personal reaction to that pressure cooker in the booth.

Or maybe, simply, I had neglected to eat properly during the past few days of tumult.

Whatever the reason, I walked into a Greek luncheonette and ordered and consumed, totally and quickly, a feta cheese omelet with french fries on the side.

But that wasn't all. I then had two cups of coffee and a large wedge of what used to be called Boston cream pie.

When I had finished stuffing myself, I pushed the plate away and fell into one of those post-gorge minidepressions.

Where, I thought, was my sense of triumph, of well-being?

I had just solved a grisly and difficult murder working with only the barest of clues. I had constructed a rather brilliant Venus flytrap and it had done its job to perfection.

And now I was about to save poor little Frenchy, a pawn in an ugly little game.

So, where was my sense of accomplishment?

I should have been flooded with it . . . I should be like Ginger Rogers tiptoeing down the street with an invisible Fred Astaire.

But there I was, at a counter in a Greek luncheonette, morose as hell and sick to my stomach.

My friend Nora's favorite Latinism popped into my head.

Omni animale post coitu triste, or something to that effect.

She always said she didn't really know how to spell it or pronounce it or really translate it—and she wasn't sure of the source, but it might be St. Augustine.

Her translation was: "After sex everyone and I mean everyone gets sad."

It didn't apply to me now. But that's what came into my head.

I walked fast to Thirty-first and Ninth.

The kennel was one of your standard New

York City pet emporiums. It sold puppies: There were two Yorkies and an English bull in one window. It sold kittens: There were four Siamese in the other windows. And it sold all kinds of pet food supplies.

I peered through the front door. In the back I could see a wall of cages. That was where, I supposed, they boarded animals.

They didn't have fish, I noted, but they did have hamsters and two large cages with constricting snakes. They were no birds.

The store seemed empty of customers. I walked inside.

An elderly woman with glasses on a neck cord and wearing a lab coat greeted me warmly.

"Just looking," I said.

I slowly worked my way to the back of the store, checking out leashes, dog bones, fake mice, feeding bowls, fancy cat litter boxes, and the newest breed books.

When I reached the cage section, I abandoned all pretense and just started searching for an abducted Russian blue.

I found Frenchy on wall three, row two, cage five.

I had to crouch down to inform her that the marines had landed and she was free.

She gave me one of her wonderful ladylike looks, as if I were a saleswoman trying to get her to sign on the dotted line for something she didn't need and would never get even if she did need and did sign.

Then she closed her eyes and resumed her nap.

I opened the cage, plucked her out, and held her close.

"We were very worried about you, Miss Blue," I purred.

"Put that cat back!"

I turned toward the shout. The woman who had spoken was incensed.

"These animals back here are not for sale. Please do not remove them from the cages."

She quickly closed the distance between us and tried to take Frenchy out of my arms.

I evaded her and stepped away. "Wait! You don't understand."

She put her glasses on her nose. "There is nothing to understand, miss. She is not for sale. Now put that cat back or there'll be trouble. You're frightening her."

"Nonsense. I'm here to pick her up."

She calmed down and scrutinized me.

"You didn't bring her in," she said.

"No," I admitted.

"Do you have a receipt?"

What an idiot I was. I forgot even to ask Anton Woburn for one. Of course, it might have been Terry Ray or even Arlene Boccio who had the receipt.

"I lost it," I said.

"I'm sorry, miss. I can't just release this cat to someone I don't know, someone who doesn't have any proof at all that she's authorized to pick up this animal."

"Then I'll just have to walk out of here without your permission," I snapped at her.

"Just you try it, miss!"

A customer had come in; he was looking at the cat carriers.

I tried to defuse the situation; to buy some time while I thought of a strategy. Frenchy was now aware that her freedom was at stake. She began to bat my right ear with her left paw.

"Look," I tried to reason with the woman, "why don't you take care of that customer over there. I'll stay right here. I promise I won't move."

A moment later the problem became academic.

The customer came over to us toting a beautiful mesh carrier with a shoulder strap. It was trimmed in genuine leather and lined in plush.

I could hardly believe my eyes. The man with the fancy carrier was A.G. Roth.

He didn't say a word to me; he didn't even look at me.

In his free hand were two hundred-dollar

bills. He thrust them at the lady proprietor. Confused, she accepted them.

Then he said, "My name is A.G. Roth. I am the lawyer for the woman who owns this cat. She—the cat, that is—was stolen from my client's premises and placed in your care. I assume you had no knowledge of this criminal act. The woman holding the cat now is said cat's contracted cat-sitter. I vouch for her. If you let her leave quietly with the animal I will forget—totally expunge it from my memory—that the stolen cat was kept here at your establishment.

"But if you do not let the woman leave with the animal, I will assume that you are, beyond a shadow of a doubt, part of a criminal conspiracy and a willing conduit for stolen property. This will cause you great grief. Do you understand?"

The woman stared at A.G. dumbfounded. Finally, she nodded her head in affirmation.

A.G. said, "Good. This cat carrier, I see, is priced at a hundred and nineteen ninety-five. The remaining eighty dollars or so will be for the cat's room and board while here. I hope it's sufficient."

Again she nodded dumbly.

A.G. opened the carrier. I placed Frenchy inside and zipped it up. A.G. tried to hoist the carrier over his shoulder. I took it from him and put it on my own shoulder.

We walked out of the store together and out to the curb.

"I got a call," he said, "from a Sam Tully. He told me about Anton Woburn. And he told me that you saw me with Rachel."

I didn't say anything. My eyes were searching the street for a cab.

"Was that why I didn't hear from you, Alice? Because of Rachel? Well, was that it? Answer me, damn you!"

"Don't raise your voice to me."

He grabbed my free arm. I shook him off.

"There is nothing between Rachel and me except a weird kind of friendship. Don't you understand? She's still a fourteen-year-old girl. I'm her surrogate father—and mother. The girl is in trouble; deranged. She attempts suicide every eighteen months. So what do I do? I squire her around. I take her to events. I buy her a gift or two on her birthday. That day you saw us, Rachel asked me to accompany her to a friend's engagement party. There is nothing remotely romantic or sexual or intimate in our relationship. She's a confused, high-strung, around-the-bend, sad young lady."

I began to feel very small. Silly. Out of touch with the world.

"I want us to be together, Alice. I don't care about anything else."

"Not now, A.G."

"If not now, when?"

"I have to return Frenchy."

"You won't get a cab now."

"Then I'll have to walk."

"It's fifty blocks."

"I'll walk," I said.

"Okay. I'll walk with you."

"No. Go home, A.G. I have to think."

"Wasn't it good with me?"

"Yes."

"Something out there threw us together, Alice. Don't mess that up. These are the only kinds of things that count."

I started to laugh, in spite of myself.

"Am I being stupid, Alice? Am I acting the fool? Is that why you're laughing at me? Is my love for you really funny?"

I couldn't tell him why I was laughing. It was the sudden peculiar insight that this strange man believed in unseen forces which had somehow brought us into bed together. A.G. was like poor dear demented Pancho, my cat who spent each night fleeing from unseen forces.

I headed uptown. A.G. was gentlemanly enough not to follow.

But he kept yelling out: "Call me! Call me!"

All I did was wave. I didn't know if I would call him. I didn't know what or how I would tell Tony about my indiscretion.

Frenchy began to mew. My gait was a bit too disjointed for her.

I settled into a slower pace. It dawned on me that there was a more pressing problem than A.G. Roth vs. Tony Basillio.

Once I delivered Frenchy back home, what in heaven's name was I going to do with Mr. Smith?

Read on for the next

Alice Nestleton Mystery . . .

A Cat on a Gargoyle

Coming in 2001

Alexander Woodward and Lila Huggins.

Do the names ring a bell?

You surely know of Burns and Allen, Eli Wallach and Ann Jackson, Lunt and Fontaine, Hume Cronyn and Jessica Tandy—to name just a few famous theatrical couples.

But Woodward and Huggins? Maybe not. Probably not.

I, however, know them and revere them. From the 1950s through the mid-1980s, they were brilliant character actors. Alone or together, they graced a hundred stages.

Their specialty was the bit parts in the imported productions—Ibsen, Chekhov, Racine, et al.—the ones that usually ran five weeks and then bye-bye.

But their fame in the theater world comes not from their acting. Not at all. They are known because they are the proprietors of a quirky little restaurant, the Red Witch, on the second floor of a rickety building on West Third Street, in Greenwich Village. Alex and Lila started it in the 1960s because they were starving. Acting work was, to say the least, scarce. The restaurant quickly became, and remains, a place where out of work actors and not a few celebrities are compelled to visit for companionship, adulation, criticism, and cheap meals.

The Red Witch is unusual in several ways. You can get coffee and snacks all day long, but real meals are only served from about 10 P.M. until 3 A.M.

And because Alex and Lila run the Red Witch like a repertory company, the quality of the meals varies wildly. A chef rarely stays on for more than three months. Some of these chefs are world class, some right out of cooking school.

The cuisine is as diverse as the quality. Early American. French. Senegalese. Jewish. Italian. American Indian. Afghani. Hungarian. To name but a few.

One of the more endearing aspects of the Red Witch is the fact that no two table settings are alike. The two starving actors outfitted the place one chair, one cup, one spoon at a time.

One of the less endearing aspects is the fact that the walls are lined with huge blowups of still photographs from the horrendous movie called *The Wake of the Red Witch:* a Hollywood seafaring extravaganza, circa 1950, which starred, among others, Gail Russell. Why did they decorate the restaurant with those photos? I never found out. Maybe Alex and Lila found them in a dumpster somewhere.

Or maybe it was just a kind of national eccentricity. After all, Alex and Lila are both English born, even though, in a profound sense, New York City bred.

I love them dearly, which is why I was trudging through the dirty snow, making my way to their apartment on that cold Sunday afternoon in February.

On this day every year their friends troop over to their West 57th Street digs—never to the Red Witch—to have coffee with them. Stale cookies are also provided.

It is the annual wedding anniversary celebration of Lila and Alex. This year, number fifty-five and counting.

No gifts brought, no alcohol served. Just a little get-together. And no one stays for very long. When I first started attending these gatherings, about eighteen years ago, there were wall-to-wall people. Death and relocation—but chiefly death—have thinned the crowd out over the years.

They live in an old red stone building between Ninth and Tenth avenues, way up on the fifth floor. There is no elevator. Alex claims that fifty percent of all climbs up result in his collapse on the second landing, where he lies unconscious for an hour and is then kicked back down the stairs by an unfriendly neighbor. Alexander has a rather macabre sense of humor.

I arrived at 2:40, was buzzed in, climbed up the five flights, and knocked on their door.

A stunning young woman answered. Forest green eyes, long black hair that fell every which way, and the body of a stripper. She was wearing spiked heels, tight overalls, a black velvet sweater, and a scarf at her neck.

I didn't know who she was. But I did intuit what she was.

In addition to hiring theater people for the restaurant, Alexander and Lila always provided room and board for out of work, out of rent actresses. Sometimes they stayed only a few days, sometimes it was weeks, and in a few instances it was much longer than that—even as long as two years. While these young women lived in the apartment, Lila characterized them as her secretary, and they did everything from cooking and cleaning to—well, to being secretaries.

"I'm Asha," the creature declared. Then, in

response to hearing my name, "Are you *the* Alice?"

"Well, I am Alice Nestleton."

"Good! Excellent! Lila has been waiting for you."

Really? I thought. Why?

Asha led me into the sprawling apartment with its beautiful wooden floors, high ceilings, and twisty hallways. The building had once been a mansion, and even after having been cut up, divided, subdivided, and degraded over the years, the apartments were still magnificent.

Passing through the living room, I saw the small circle of guests surrounding the seated Alexander, who was holding court as usual.

I spotted a photographer I knew—Brad Carmody.

And a musician named Lister.

And the baker Nozak, who supplied the Red Witch with breads and pastries.

Asha led me to the study and vanished after she ushered me in.

I had been in this room before. Nothing but four walls of bookcases, two large easy chairs at opposite ends of the room, and a very thick rug.

"My dear Alice! You always look so splendid in the cold weather. I do believe you are that rarest of creatures—a winter woman. Of course, if I recall, you are from the harsh climate of North Dakota."

"Minnesota," I corrected her, laughing. She looked good. Rather, she looked no older or wearier than she had last year.

"Do you find it peculiar that I am lying on the floor, Alice?"

Actually she was sitting on the rug, legs extended at arthritic angles.

What I did find "peculiar" was that she was wearing pajamas.

"Sit down. Join me," she said, patting the rug.

"I thought I would just say hello to Alexander first. Then I'll come back," I said. I really did not care to sprawl out on the floor, truth be told.

"But you'll miss the floor show," she moaned.

"What floor show?"

"Just come down here beside me for a minute."

I lowered myself onto the rug, not a little annoyed.

Suddenly, from the back of one of the chairs, came two little cannonballs, hurtling toward me.

One tumbled and rolled over, then quickly recovered and joined the other.

A second later, two adorable orange tabby kittens were sliding up and down my arms and legs.

"Alice, I want you to meet Billy and Bob. Don't ask me which is which."

"When did you get them?" I asked in delight.

"A few days ago."

"*Where* did you get them?"

"Oh, I have my sources," she said.

The kittens had another burst of energy, then jumped off me and collapsed, as kittens will. I watched them as they snoozed.

"I spend hours with them," Lila admitted. "Alex thinks I've gone around the bend."

"Doesn't he like cats?"

"Grudgingly, Alice. He says he gets exhausted watching them. He says they remind him of Bob Fosse. You do know Bob Fosse, don't you, dear?"

"Yes, sure. Although I never worked with him. Besides, Lila, he's dead. For some years now."

She cocked her head and appeared to be contemplating something I had said. Then she began slowly to get to her feet. "Come. Let us join the crowd."

We slipped out of the room, closing the door softly behind us, and walked into the living room.

Alexander was still addressing his subjects. Lila walked to his chair and sat on its arm.

She kissed him lovingly on the top of his head.

It was a simple, natural gesture . . . so common . . . seemingly without passion or importance . . . or anything.

It was just a mundane expression of friendship and intimacy between people who had lived together a very long time—in bad times and good.

No one in the room gave a second thought to that kiss.

Except me.

It jolted me severely, in head and heart.

It filled me with longing and dread.

Longing? Yes! Because in a sense that was what I craved . . . that was the relationship I had always craved with a man.

Dread? Yes! Because it dawned on me right there and then that I would never have it.

Surely not soon.

My man troubles had escalated to such an extent that I had decided on a temporary refuge: chastity.

My long-time lover, Tony Basillio, and I were now just friends.

My last extra-Basillio affair—the gentleman in question was one A.G. Roth—was passionate but brief. Upon termination it had also transformed into a curious kind of friendship.

I was very close to mawkish tears.

Alexander had now moved into his story of "nuptial origins," as he put it.

I had heard it before. At least eighteen times before.

In fact I knew it by heart. But, like the others, I listened, because, as critics used to say, "Alexander Woodward could make the telephone book sound like *Othello*."

The time is the 1940s. They are both young, English, and in New York, but they do not know each other.

They both get bit parts in a G. B. Shaw play.

Alexander falls head over heels in love with her.

She finds him obnoxious.

To entice her to his apartment he claims to be a great chef, and the son of a great chef. He invites her to dinner again and again. Again and again she refuses.

Finally she relents, and shows up with a friend.

Alexander, in fact, can cook only four things: omelets; mushrooms fried in butter and topped with sour cream; flank steak with onions; tapioca pudding.

He decides against the omelets and prepares the other three dishes for his guest.

At the end of the dinner, Lila announces it was one of the five worst meals of her life.

But she adds the dictum. "Any man who cooks so hard and so badly must have a heart of pure gold."

The story, once finished, was greeted with applause, as always.

I stayed for another half hour, chatting with the others and revisiting the kittens.

Then I said good-bye to Alex and Lila, promising to visit the kittens often.

Outside, despite the powerful sun, the cold wind was whipping up litter.

I felt wonderful, my brief bout of tears aside. I always felt good after my visit to that couple.

I started walking east on Fifty-seventh, into the wind.

Half a block later, the wildest and most delicious idea surfaced.

It was a non-Nestletonian idea, to be sure, and it would never have occurred to me had I not been relatively affluent at the time.

Let me explain:

I had just completed work on a pilot for an independent TV producer who was trying to sell a series to the networks. It was a cop show—aren't they all. But with a difference. The producer figured that in a market saturated with such shows he would go back in time and do a

"Broadway beat" cop show, situated in the 1950s. The series would be called *Broadway: Bad & Beautiful.*

I played—would you believe it—a world weary actress turned bartender!

Only a bit, of course, but I was $5,000 richer than I'd been last week.

So, my idea was simple. A gift for a wonderful old theatrical couple. No one had ever been allowed to bring them an anniversary present; they forbade it.

But this gift they would accept. How could they not?

I would send them a replica of the meal that eventually led to the nuptials. My friend Nora's restaurant, the Pal Joey Bistro, was only a few blocks away. I was so happy at conceiving the idea that I virtually skipped all the way there.

Nora didn't have any time for me. A tour group was booked in for late brunch. But I pulled her aside for a moment and asked for help.

Could her chef prepare mushrooms fried in butter and topped with sour cream, flank steak with onions, and tapioca pudding?

Could she have it delivered in an hour or two?

My friend Nora looked at me as if I were demented.

"Who would eat such a mess?" she asked.

"Eighty-five-year-old lovebirds."

Chaos was erupting all around us. Nora's staff was just not used to serving a full contingent for Sunday brunch.

"Okay, okay," she said. She pulled me to the bar and thrust a pencil and pad into my hand. "Write it all down, Alice. The dishes. The name and address."

"I am going to pay for this, Nora."

"Damn right you are. Plus a ten dollar delivery charge. And if my chef quits over this order, you'll pay damages also."

Then she grinned, kissed me on the cheek and rushed back into the fray.

She stopped in her tracks suddenly, turned, and asked, "Are you serious? Tapioca?"

"Yes."

"You poor child," she said, and fled.

I went home, still high from my brilliant idea. I went to a French movie starring a favorite actor of mine: Michel Piccoli. An old man now, but still a wonderful presence. But my, has he gotten fat.

I ate alone in a Moroccan restaurant on Bedford Street. It was delicious, except for the amorous waiter.

When I got back home I brushed my Maine

coon cat, Bushy, and tried to do the same for Pancho, the crazy one. No luck.

The phone rang at 10:14. For some reason I noted the exact time.

Lila Huggins was on the other end of the line. She was bubbling over with joy.

"We have eaten every scrap of that horrendous meal, Alice. It was the sweetest gift we have ever received from anyone. Bless you, dear. Alex sends his love. And so do Billy and Bob."

With that, she hung up.

I had never been happier in my life.

Then things turned, to use Lila's word, peculiar.

Exactly twelve hours later, meaning at 10:14 A.M. on the following day, I received a call from someone identifying herself as Asha.

She was hysterical.

It took me a few minutes to remember who she was.

She was calling from Roosevelt Hospital, she said. Both Lila Huggins and Alexander Woodward had been taken to the emergency room at eleven o'clock the previous evening.

Lila had died at seven in the morning.

Alex was still alive, but critically ill and in intensive care.

Asha hung up. I sat there, dazed.

Ten minutes later, there was another phone call from another hysterical woman.

Nora.

It seems that one of her waiters had stepped out for a smoke at two in the morning and a lunatic waiting in the alley had pumped five bullets into his head.

Odder still was the fact that the murdered waiter was the one who had delivered the anniversary meal to Lila and Alexander.